DATE DUE 842612

28 DAYS

Cohen, Anthea
Angel of vengeance

Angel of Vengeance

By Anthea Cohen

ANGEL OF VENGEANCE
ANGEL WITHOUT MERCY
ANGEL OF DEATH

Angel of Vengeance

ANTHEA COHEN

PUBLISHED FOR THE CRIME CLUB BY
DOUBLEDAY & COMPANY, INC.
GARDEN CITY, NEW YORK
1984

All of the characters in this book
are fictitious, and any resemblance
to actual persons, living or dead,
is purely coincidental.

Library of Congress Cataloging in Publication Data

Cohen, Anthea.
Angel of vengeance.

I. Title.
PR6053.O34A76   1984   823'.914
ISBN: 0-385-19126-X
Library of Congress Catalog Card Number 83-25512
Copyright © 1982 by Anthea Cohen
All Rights Reserved
Printed in the United States of America
First Edition in the United States of America

Angel of Vengeance

1

Sister Carmichael sat in her glass office in the middle of Out Patients, the hot, late-August sunshine warming, almost to the point of discomfort, the back of her head and shoulders. She sniffed . . . opened one of the drawers of her desk, drew out a man-sized tissue, and blew her nose violently. It did little to relieve the congestion. Sister Carmichael was, as usual, suffering from her yearly bout of hay fever. She got up irritably, opening the window at the back of her office overlooking the flowered square which acted as St. Matthew's Hospital garden.

She stood for a moment, gazing out at the small lawn and flowered borders divided into four by flagged paths. Dried-out-looking teak slatted seats were placed at intervals round the lawn, the back of each seat bearing the name of the benefactor.

Sister Carmichael turned away from the window; the pollen from the flowers would make her hay fever worse. She doubted the wisdom of opening the window at all, but it was so hot in the office, and it seemed the lesser of two evils. She blew her nose again, then surreptitiously opened another drawer and took out a small mirror and looked down at herself. The picture was not prepossessing.

Since leaving her last hospital, St. Jude's, Carmichael had made a lot of effort to change her image, had bought new make-up, tried even a coloured rinse on her hair, but the red-rimmed eyes and the pink-tipped long nose remained disappointingly apparent. Her fawn hair was now done up in a bun at the nape of her neck, the rest of her hair scraped back severely. She shook her head and frowned, and put the mirror back in the drawer.

Nurses flitted to and fro among the six clinic rooms, each flanked by four examination rooms. A medical secretary passed her office and smiled pleasantly; Carmichael nodded in return. The secretary stopped and put her head round the door. "Good morning, Sister Carmichael," she said, cheerfully. "Oh, are you in the throes? Isn't hay fever the end? I've got a friend with it, he nearly goes berserk, so does his mother having to wash all his handkerchiefs." She smiled again and disappeared into the clinic room opposite Carmichael's office.

Sister Carmichael was not pleased. It must be very obvious, her hay fever; she did not wish it to be. She opened the drawer again, took out her compact, glanced around hastily, and dabbed powder on her nose and upper lip. It was useless, she knew that; her make-up was quickly destroyed by the constant blowing of her nose.

She looked at the big electric clock in the waiting-room, half past nine. The coloured plastic chairs were filling up as patients came through the front door of the department and waited in front of the records office, with its sliding glass window. They waited to report their presence, their names and addresses, and, in some cases, their numbers, if they knew them.

It was easy to tell the old hands from the new patients; they smiled, and nodded, and chatted familiarly with the young girl at the records desk, while the others, the new ones, looked round them, nervously, hesitantly gave their names and addresses, then waited for directions where to sit.

The waiting-room was pleasant, and Carmichael gazed at it critically. The chairs were grouped round small tables on which were magazines, a large No Smoking notice obviated the need for ashtrays. In the corner was a small canteen, serving tea, coffee, Ovaltine, Horlicks, and chocolate biscuits and crisps.

At that moment the tea-lady came in, waved her hand across at Sister Carmichael, opened the flap of the canteen, went inside, divested herself of her outdoor cardigan, and slipped on a green overall.

The telephone rang. Carmichael picked it up and sneezed. A voice at the other end said: "Stuart Martin here. Sister, will you tell my Registrar I shall be slightly delayed, and tell him to start the clinic, and if there's anything he's worried about, hold them back for me. Right?"

Before Carmichael had time to recover from her sneeze and again wipe her dripping nose, the phone was put down. A little delayed, Carmichael sneered. In the three months she'd been at St. Matthew's, Mr. Stuart Martin, Senior Consultant Surgeon, had been "a little delayed" at each clinic. She wondered why he had taken the trouble to ring up—probably because he would be later than ever this morning.

At that moment Dr. Rai, the Surgical Registrar, of whom Mr. Stuart Martin had spoken, walked through the back door of the department and passed Carmichael's desk towards his clinic room, with his House Officer following him. Rai waved a friendly hand at Carmichael; his companion looked ahead, giving no greeting. He looked sleepy and cross. They both disappeared into the surgical clinic talking in a low monotone.

Sister Carmichael rose to follow them in to relay the message that had just come to them from their chief. As she approached the consulting-room door, she heard the House Officer, Philip Marks, say to Rai: "I don't know why they appointed her; she looks like a bloody goldfish in a bowl, sitting there with her mouth open. I don't see why Holly Newman couldn't have got the job, she was well suited for it in my opinion. Patients like to see someone pretty when they come up here; it's bad enough for them having to come anyway."

Carmichael stood frozen outside the door. She had heard every word. Dr. Rai turned round and saw her. "Oh, Sister Carmichael, good morning," he said lamely, glancing at Philip Marks with a frown. But the House Officer moved across the consulting room to his chair situated in the corner, where he was to sit and listen and learn. He didn't look at the Out Patients' Sister.

"Mr. Stuart Martin has just telephoned and said he will be slightly delayed, Mr. Rai." Carmichael looked directly at him, and he looked directly back at her; she could tell by his expression that he was embarrassed.

"Oh, thank you, Sister Carmichael. Did he say that I was to get on with it and keep anything back that I was worried about? That's his usual message." He was trying to be pleasant, but Carmichael would have none of it; she merely nodded and went back to her office. She sat for a few moments thinking of the remark. Well, we shall see; young doctors shouldn't cross Sisters as blatantly as that, she thought. She got up, straightened her shoulders, smiled slightly, blew her nose violently on another tissue which she popped into her pocket, then left her office to walk round the other five clinics to see that they were all properly laid up, and that the nurses were ready to receive the physician, the orthodontist, the orthopaedic surgeon and the usual midweek morning clinic consultants.

In the surgical clinic room, Rai turned to the House Officer: "She heard you, you know, Phil. It was a silly thing to say. After all, an Out Patients' Sister, it's best to keep on the right side of them, they can make things unpleasant if you're not careful."

"How? I don't give a damn for her," said Philip Marks,

flicking through the notes on his lap. "Besides, I think they should have appointed Holly."

"Well, it's not up to us, it's up to the appointments committee. And everybody knew that Holly opened her legs too easily, that's why she didn't get the job," said Rai.

The secretary on the other side of the room, in a corner, fixing up her typewriter and shuffling her papers together, tut-tutted, then smiled. "Come on now, Phil, you shouldn't have said that, it was a nasty thing to say. Carmichael's got rotten hay fever, that's why she has to breathe through her mouth like that. And you, Dr. Rai, shouldn't say things like that about Holly, so both of you be quiet," she smiled pleasantly, and the smile took the sting from the reprimand she obviously thought she must give the two doctors.

"Where did she come from anyway?" Phil Marks asked. "She looks as if she crawled out of the woodwork."

"Shut up and let's get on with it," said Rai, and at that moment a nurse walked in. "Ready for the first patient? I hear the great man is going to be late, that makes a change," the nurse grinned, widely, and the atmosphere of tension was reduced as Dr. Rai sat down in front of the desk, opened the first case notes, and read the doctor's letter.

"Query appendix. I think I can just manage that." He looked at the age of the patient. "Hmm, age twenty-two, yeah, all right, wheel her in." The nurse went to the door and called the patient's name, and the clinic started.

2

Mr. Stuart Martin arrived exactly one hour late. He nodded at Carmichael as he passed her office, but did not wait for any acknowledgement of the salute. He turned into his clinic room; Carmichael got up and went to the records office. It wasn't her job to collect the notes; there was a clerk in the department specially laid on for this, but there was something Carmichael wanted to do. She collected a pile of four notes that had accumulated on the shelf in front of the records-office glass window for the surgical clinic and brought them back to her own office. Once inside, she flicked open the buff folders and took from one a set of notes. These she placed on her desk. She walked into the clinic room with the folders, three full and one empty, and put them down in front of the secretary, and retired, but not out of earshot.

The next patient came in and went out, and Carmichael still hovered near the clinic room door; then an old patient, a follow-up, was ushered in. Stuart Martin took the folder and opened it, and Carmichael heard him say: "The folder is empty. For God's sake, where are the notes? Did you write them up?" He turned to Philip Marks. "Did you write them up? You must have put them back in the wrong folder. The wrong folder, for God's sake! Can't you see the clinic is ready before I get here?"

His irritation seemed to be focused mainly on the House Surgeon, though such a fault could arise elsewhere, but

Carmichael was aware there was no love lost between Mr. Stuart Martin and the young man.

After allowing another few minutes to elapse and hearing the consultant's voice rise in anger, Carmichael walked into the clinic room with the missing notes in her hand, her face apologetic, the end of her pink nose twitching as it did in times of triumph or stress; this time it was undoubtedly triumph. "Oh, Mr. Martin, these notes were in my office, on top of my file, I didn't notice them. It was only when I heard you call the patient in, nurse, that I realized . . . Dr. Marks must have left them there when he . . ."

Phil Marks' mouth opened in quick protest, but before he could speak, Stuart Martin forestalled him. "Thanks, Sister." He turned to his House Officer. "You really should be more careful, Marks," he said. "This is how notes get lost. It can hold up the entire clinic; you must learn to be more methodical. After all, if a doctor hasn't got method, he's nothing."

Carmichael's red-rimmed eyes met those of Dr. Philip Marks. He glared back at her; he got the picture immediately. Bitch, he thought. Carmichael's long look at him ended; she dropped the inflamed lids behind her glasses and walked quietly out of the clinic. Stuart Martin got up and went into the examination room, and as he did so, Carmichael heard Rai say: "I told you, Phil. Out Patient Sisters are people to be wary of, they've got ways and means. They can make a clinic go smoothly, or rough as hell."

Mr. Stuart Martin turned round at the examination room door. "I beg your pardon, did you say anything, Rai?" Rai shook his head, and Carmichael continued on her way back to her office. Yes indeed, you have to be careful of me, she thought, not only of Out Patient Sisters, but more especially of me.

Even as this thought crossed her mind, she felt a vague

unhappiness—depression. Why? She sought for the reason as she sat there at her desk, fighting back the inevitable sneeze.

When she had left her last hospital, she had exuded confidence, confidence that had come suddenly, like a new character being transfused into her . . . She knew, she knew why. The death of Marion Hughes had made her feel godlike, supreme, and that feeling had brought with it a benign attitude to others. At the interview for this post she had sounded to herself, and obviously to the interviewers, a pleasant, capable, likeable woman. Why then the change? Why the feeling that she was not only receding back to the old Carmichael, but assuming something within her of Marion Hughes . . . Of her nastiness, her hostility . . . Even to herself she knew she was not as pleasant as she had been when the post had started three months before. Her attitude to the doctors, too, was changing; she could feel it, the feeling of uncertainty, that they were humiliating her, looking down on her, thinking that she was socially not their equal. That was the old Carmichael; why? She felt like the sand on the shore when the tide's going out; it's left wet and shining, then dries into the original dull sand. What did she need to put it right, to moisten it, make it fresh and gleaming again? Another . . . ? No, she shook her head. She was thinking like a psychopath. That didn't answer the question though. She must be more pleasant to the staff, not play little tricks like she had just done on the House Surgeon. That was not even the old Carmichael; that was more like Marion Hughes, the hated, loathed, destroyed Marion Hughes. Perhaps she was not destroyed, perhaps she was living again in Carmichael, perhaps she needed another act like that to obliterate Marion Hughes completely from her mind. Carmichael shook her head, and a patient she had not noticed, standing in her office doorway, spoke to her. "Penny for them, Sister, you shook your head very disapprovingly then."

Carmichael looked up, her eyes vacant, then focused them on the woman in front of her. She was middle-aged, well preserved, good-looking.

"Oh, good morning." Carmichael got up, the thought in her mind of being more pleasant still there. "Can I help you? Who are you to see?"

"Oh, I only looked round the door to say good morning. Mrs. Andrews, do you remember? My eye has gone again." She looked at Carmichael through two very bright blue eyes and it was difficult to know what she meant; Carmichael tilted her head sideways, questioningly. "I'm sorry to hear that. Gone again?" she asked.

"Yes, that's right. My retina. The sky's covered with little black dots, I know the signs. Frightens me to death. I've come to see him." She jerked her head in the direction of the eye clinic.

"Well, you couldn't see anyone better. Have you reported at the office?" said Carmichael, and she liked the sound of herself, and repeated, "You couldn't see anyone better than Mr. Ealing."

The woman nodded. "I know, but it frightens you, I mean, I read it up, and if your retina . . . well, you can go blind, you know." She blinked at Carmichael through her glasses and pointed out into the garden. "It's not so bad when I look at the grass, but when I look at the sky, it's, well, like polka dots." She laughed, nervously.

Carmichael nodded. "Very worrying for you, but let's go down to the eye clinic. Can you see all right to walk down the corridor?" she asked.

The woman nodded. "Oh, yes, I can see all right, but it's, well, you know, you're a nurse," she said, and Carmichael nodded.

Actually Carmichael had done a very short time in the eye

department in her general training. She had confessed this blithely and confidently at her interview, and it had made no difference. Her manner, her pleasantness and honesty had obviously impressed the interviewers. They had flipped through her papers and told her it was just a question of references. These must have been good, for she had got the job.

Having walked with the patient round to the eye department, she sat in the small waiting-room reserved for eye patients only. It was separate from the big room, in case any of them should not be able to see very well. The eye nurse looked up as Carmichael brought the patient; she smiled and Carmichael smiled back. Then she went back to her office, feeling that she had conquered a little bit of the old Carmichael, but she was still not sure of herself. Perhaps she was lonely, perhaps she should look for a friend among the Sisters in the hospital; she really had had little to do with them as yet. Yes, she thought, maybe that was it—she should look for a friend, to take her out of herself, to talk to. Or, should she look for an enemy? After all, it was that that had helped her before.

3

In the children's ward, the paediatrician and the Sister in charge were standing beside a cot, in which lay a rather undersized, thin little three-year-old girl. Her round blue eyes stared up at them fearfully, and she lay quite still, her arms stretched rigidly outside the covers. She looked tense and frightened. On the right side of her head, stretching from hair-line to temple, was a large, swollen bruise.

"What do you think, Sister?" The paediatrician, Dr. Stephenson, looked inquiringly at Sister, and Sister looked back at him with a set mouth and unyielding expression. "I think the child's been hit, I'm sure of it. Something should be done; we can't send her home, not until we know."

"We may have to, Sister, if the parents demand it. We've no proof at all."

"A broken leg, a broken arm, and now this. She must be very accident-prone." Sister's voice was acid.

"I know, but after all, children do fall, and they say the arm was broken in the nursery-school playground."

Sister nodded automatically.

"Well, we'll have a full skeletal X-ray. I'm not going to let the child go home without. If we find anything else, well . . . The Social Services have already been alerted?"

"Of course. They tried to find the neighbour who had said she had heard Marie screaming late at night, and sometimes during the day. Apparently the woman's moved and they can't trace her. All very unsatisfactory, I hate this kind of case." Sister Jones, the children's ward Sister, loved children beyond anything else, and her face showed the concern she felt as she looked down at the child.

"So do I." The paediatrician spoke wearily. "Well, I'm seeing the father after clinic tomorrow, maybe it's as well if we get that X-ray done this morning; if there's anything else showing, old fractures or anything, we'll be on safer ground, I can talk to him more firmly."

"Meanwhile, we'll keep the child in as long as we can, on any pretext, I think," the Sister suggested.

"I suppose so, but there's nothing really to . . . not unless we find something more on X-ray. Let's put it off until we've done that."

"All right, Dr. Stephenson." Sister looked at him resentfully as he turned away from the cot. He was weak, she thought, not like Dr. Braithwaite, who would have stood no nonsense. He wouldn't have let the kid go home under any circumstances, even if he suspected . . . But then, this new paediatrician, she supposed he didn't want to blot his copy-book. She accompanied him to the next bed, in which a baby bounced up and down, his nappy sliding down his legs. He smiled and held out his arms to Dr. Stephenson, who went up to him gratefully. "How's this baby's eczema?" he asked.

"Much better at the moment. It comes and goes," and Sister noticed with what relief Dr. Stephenson left little Marie Abbott. It was obvious he didn't like dealing with problems unless they were purely medical. Well, she'd do her damnedest to keep the kid in, that was for sure. At that moment the House Physician came in, breathless, and approached Dr. Stephenson. "Sorry I'm late, sir. I had to go and look at an eye in Casualty."

Dr. Stephenson nodded absently. "I see. What do you think of little Marie Abbott there?" He motioned towards the child's cot.

"I don't know," said the House Physician. "Don't like the

look of it terribly. Broken leg, broken arm, and then this. Better watch it, I suppose." He looked at Sister for guidance, and she nodded adamantly.

"Certainly, we'd better watch it," she said.

4

Sister Carmichael watched the last patient departing from the afternoon clinic. She looked at the clock; twenty past five. In theory, at five o'clock the department closed, but often the clinics ran slightly later. Today the last mother and child had disappeared from the paediatric clinic and the young House Physician, a timid woman Carmichael rather liked, came out of the clinic room and put her head round Sister's office door.

"Sister Carmichael, a Mr. Abbott"—she looked at the note in her hand—"actually it's Major Abbott, or that's what he's down as here, is coming to see Dr. Stephenson about his kid on the children's ward. It's a special interview, you know, so I shan't stay." She nodded her head towards the clinic room. "He wants to be alone with the father to have a chat, so I'm off." She hitched the large bundle of notes under her arm and disappeared towards the Medical Secretary's offices.

Dr. Stephenson emerged from the clinic room and spoke to Carmichael: "Did she say," he said in his vague, rather indeterminate way, "did she say this chap Abbott was coming? Sorry about it, but I thought it was better to have him here when the rest had gone."

Carmichael nodded. "Yes, that's right, the nurses can go, I'll wait," she said.

"There's no need at all for you to wait." Dr. Stephenson looked at her.

"I prefer to. While there are people in the department, I

prefer to be here." Carmichael's voice was adamant, and Stephenson was not the kind of man to argue with such a tone. He nodded, turned back into the clinic room, and Carmichael watched him. He stooped unnecessarily, as if he were afraid of banging his head on the doors, which were adequate, even for his six foot two. This, although he was a young man, gave him a natural stoop. He carried his head on one side in a propitiating manner, which made Carmichael dislike him.

At 5:30 precisely a man walked through the doors from the street into Out Patients. He was of medium height, with a military air about him. He came up to Carmichael's office and she got up and went to greet him. "Major Abbott?" she said, and the man beamed.

"Major Abbott it is, Sister," he said. "I'm here to have a chat with the old doc—Stephenson, isn't it?"

Carmichael became slightly colder in her manner. "Dr. Stephenson," she said pointedly, but the point seemed completely lost on Abbott, who went on beaming.

"Please sit down, and I'll tell Dr. Stephenson you're here." Carmichael went through into the clinic room, where Dr. Stephenson was sitting, his hands clasped on the blotter in front of him, staring vacantly out of the window, Marie Abbott's notes in front of him.

"Major Abbott is here, Dr. Stephenson. Shall I show him in?" said Carmichael.

"Oh, yes, please do, and shut the door, will you?"

Sister Carmichael looked at him pointedly. "I certainly will shut the door, Dr. Stephenson," she said. "But I don't think you have anything to worry about, I'm the only one left in the department."

"Of course, of course, I didn't mean that." Stephenson was obviously cursing himself for his unfortunate remark. It was apparent to Carmichael that he liked to keep on the right side of everyone he had to work with. She tossed her head a little and walked out, back into the waiting-room.

"Major Abbott, will you please come in?" she said in a precise voice, and then spoilt the whole thing by giving a tremendous sneeze.

"Hay fever, Sister, or got a bad cold? Hope you don't give it to me." The major was very hearty, but Carmichael refused to answer. She showed him into the consulting room, where he sat down in a chair beside the desk, and, looking pointedly at Dr. Stephenson, she closed the door behind her, but she didn't move—the very fact that Dr. Stephenson wanted the door closed had made her curious. The two men started to talk; Carmichael, standing just outside the door, her ear as close as possible, listened.

5

Dr. Stephenson rose to his feet as the father of Marie Abbott walked into the consulting room. "Mr. Abbott?" he said, gesturing to the chair beside the desk.

"Major Abbott, if you don't mind, old man." Abbott's voice was loud, self-assured. He put out his hand, accepting what he took to be Dr. Stephenson's proffered handshake. The grasp was firm, almost pointedly so. He turned round, looked at the chair indicated, hitched up his trousers and sat down, crossing one knee over the other, putting his hand up and smoothing the underside of his moustache. Then his hand went toward his jacket pocket.

"Mind if I smoke? I see there's a No Smoking notice out there, but I see there's an ashtray on your desk, doc; do as I say, don't do as I do, eh?" He lighted the cigarette before Stephenson had had time to reply.

"I don't smoke actually, it wouldn't do with children coming in here," said Stephenson mildly. The man had rather taken him off his guard by his easy acceptance of the situation. Stephenson was momentarily nonplussed; he hated this. Again before he had time to speak, Abbott cut in. "Want to talk to me about my kid, then? Fire away, the wife's expecting to have her home tomorrow, or the day after, O.K.? Fit is she? Not any worse? No fractured skull or anything like that, eh?"

Dr. Stephenson turned away, faced the wall in front of him and put his hands together, thinking how to start the conversation. This time Abbott did not forestall him.

"Yes, I did want to see you. It's just the fact that your little girl seems to be so accident-prone; first the leg, then the arm, and now this, and we have had an X-ray done and found two healed fractured ribs; might have been some time ago."

Major Abbott gazed with his hard, brown eyes at Dr. Stephenson for some time, and it was some seconds before he answered. "What are you suggesting?"

There was a slight menace in his voice which Stephenson was quick to notice and quick to shy away from. "There is a condition that children suffer from called *fragilitas ossium;* it means that their bones are unusually fragile. The child doesn't present any of the symptoms or signs. There is a tendency for the whites of the eyes to be slightly blue in these cases, and this isn't present with your daughter. Nevertheless . . ." He tailed off, lamely, noticing a visible relaxing in Major Abbott.

"Oh, I see, Doctor, I see; and you think my daughter may be suffering from this disease. Is there any cure, any treatment?"

"We would like to do some more investigations on her." Dr. Stephenson obviously saw a heaven-sent opportunity of keeping the child in and therefore placating the children's ward Sister as well as the man in front of him.

"Can't she have that done as an out-patient; these tests, I mean?" Major Abbott recrossed his legs, not forgetting to pull the neat crease in his trousers up as he did so. "I mean, does she have to stay in hospital? Her mother's wanting her home, you know. She didn't come today, because, well, you did rather specify that you wanted to see me, and I thought that there was some danger to the child that you wanted to keep from her mother. Indeed, perhaps this is why you suggested I came alone; this disease, is it common?"

"We're not at all sure that she's suffering from it. Of course, maybe it's . . ."

"Maybe it's . . . what?" Major Abbott cut in.

"It could be that the child is accident-prone, and it's just coincidental. But of course, the bruise on the head, and there is a hair-line fracture of the skull, that doesn't quite fit in with . . ." Stephenson saw Major Abbott tense up again.

"Oh, just what does it fit in with then, Doctor?" Abbott asked, his eyes fixed firmly on Stephenson.

"Well, one has got to take into consideration that the child may have been hit."

Abbott jumped to his feet like an uncoiled spring. "Are you suggesting . . . You'd better be careful, Doctor, what you're saying." He remained standing and Stephenson rose as well. "I'm not suggesting anything, Major Abbott, it is just that the child has received several injuries and we must see to it that these injuries are properly explained and accurately diagnosed. If she is suffering from the complaint I have suggested, then of course precautions will have to be taken."

"Surely you know that one of the injuries was sustained in the nursery-school playground? Is that supposed to be something to do with me?"

"You are taking this far too personally, Major Abbott." Dr. Stephenson's voice was placatory. "No one, particularly me, is suggesting anything at this juncture; we would just like to do more tests."

"In view of what you have said, Doctor, I would like to take my child home as we arranged, tomorrow. I will bring her up here, of course, for any investigation you wish, but my wife and I would like her home."

Stephenson raised his hand, palm upward, and shrugged his shoulders. "That is as you wish, Major Abbott. Whatever you say about this, we will do, that is your right as a parent, but I would like to suggest that it would be much easier for us to continue the investigation whilst the child is in hospital."

"No. I intend to take her home. I've had enough of this. I can take her up to London and get this investigated properly."

"It will be investigated properly here." Dr. Stephenson's voice was firmer. "But it is, of course, as you wish, you are the parent."

"Is that why that woman came round asking questions, then? We wondered, and this has confirmed my suspicions. Very well, Doctor, I feel that I would like to withdraw my daughter entirely from your supervision."

"That would be a very foolish thing to do." Stephenson's voice, for once, was louder and more adamant.

"Foolish it may be, but after all, I can go anywhere I like, remember that, see anyone I like."

"I assure you that if you want a second opinion, I will recommend someone, or you can pick your own specialist."

Major Abbott had, by this time, got his hand on the handle of the consulting-room door and was ready to leave. "We'll call for Marie tomorrow, at ten o'clock in the morning; that's the time that Sister suggested the last time we took her home. Will you make that known to the ward, Doctor?" Major Abbott's face was white.

"I can't understand your attitude, Major Abbott. I have only suggested that your child might have a bone disease."

"Or might be being beaten up, by me."

"Don't you think you are over-reacting a little?" Dr. Stephenson's voice was urgent, but at that moment Major Abbott wrenched open the door and turned for a parting shot. "Ten o'clock tomorrow morning we'll be collecting her. Please see that they have her ready to go home." He left the consulting room, almost colliding with Carmichael. She beat a hasty retreat through the door of the corridor leading to the consulting and examination rooms.

"Going, Major Abbott?" she said innocently, and Abbott looked at her, a sneer on his face.

"Listening outside the door, Sister. Well, you might be useful as a witness, though I thought Sisters were far too dignified to do that sort of thing."

Carmichael's face flushed a deep red and she didn't answer, but stood watching Major Abbott stride through the waiting-room, fling open the swing doors, and disappear into the road outside. She was still standing as she listened to the crash of the car door shutting and the revving up of the engine as he drove off. She was trembling slightly. The flush had receded from her face, leaving it white. But she was not shaking with fear, she was shaking with rage.

Dr. Stephenson came out into the waiting-room—he looked nervously at Carmichael. "What did he say?" he asked.

"Nothing . . . nothing of importance."

"I hope he's not going to make trouble; that type of man can be dangerous," said Stephenson, beginning to take off his white coat.

"Especially to a three-year-old," said Carmichael, acidly, but she was speaking to herself. Stephenson had disappeared into the clinic room to put on his jacket. He came out, jerking his shoulders to get the coat comfortable. He took the stethoscope that Carmichael handed him. He had left it in the pocket of his white coat. "Good night, Sister," he said.

Carmichael did not answer.

6

"Mind if I sit here?" Carmichael looked up from the book she had propped up beside her plate—a large, thick book entitled *Surgery for Nurses*.

"No, of course not." Carmichael invariably chose a table in the canteen that was deserted. After three months she had not made any friends at St. Matthew's; she knew only too well that she was not the kind of person that people sought out as a companion. She was fairly happy to be alone, but on the other hand quite welcomed the children's ward Sister, who now placed a plate, knife, and fork on the table and sat down opposite her.

Sister Jones was a buxom, fresh-faced woman with, when she smiled, surprisingly yellow teeth. She raised bushy eyebrows at Carmichael, twisted her neck to one side so that she could read the title of the book beside the Out Patients Sister's plate.

"Surgery for Nurses, for God's sake," she said. "Not still studying, are you? Once I passed my exams, I vowed never to read another medical book. I have to look things up sometimes, of course, but not as a lunchtime tome. I'd rather have a romantic novel." She laughed and Carmichael smiled back at her, her reserved, downward smile.

"Don't mean to interrupt you though." The children's ward Sister gazed curiously at Carmichael. She'd hardly spoken to her since she had been appointed; for once, nobody in the hospital had appeared to have anything to say about the new Out Patients Sister; usually they had plenty about anyone new. The non-appointment of Holly, well, that had been something, but like all hospital sensations, it had soon died down. A week after Holly had disappeared to another hospital, her name had been forgotten, or almost so.

"Liking it here . . . ? What are these bloody kidneys like?" She looked down at her plate at the meat surrounded by rice. "Oh, you haven't got that, what have you got?" She looked at Carmichael's plate; she was obviously interested in and fond of food.

"Oh, I had the macaroni cheese. I wasn't feeling particularly hungry." Carmichael's red-rimmed eyes gazed across at the children's ward Sister's meal without a great deal of interest.

"Oh, you've got hay fever, have you, or is it a cold? Something putting you off your food?"

"Hay fever," said Carmichael coldly, and took a tissue out of her pocket and wiped the tip of her nose.

"Horrible. I used to have it myself at one time, then it went away. Age, I expect, the psychiatrists say it's psychological. They would . . . Anyway, once you get over forty . . ." The children's ward Sister attacked her kidneys and rice with gusto. "You didn't answer," she said. "Do you like it here; getting on all right with them?" She motioned towards the end of the canteen the consultants frequented. "That mob over there. After all, you have to handle everybody. Thank God, I only have old Stephenson and the House Physician, and the surgical men, of course, now and again; but to have the whole lot—couldn't take it. Which hospital did you come from, first Sister's post? Hear you took Holly's flat, is that right?"

"Yes." Carmichael used one word to answer the entire volley of questions shot at her.

Jones laughed easily. "Serve me bloody well right; Nosy

Parker, I am," she said, chewing on the kidneys and speaking through them.

Carmichael was not particularly impressed with her companion's table manners, but she suddenly remembered she'd got something to ask Jones. "You've got that little girl in, haven't you; Marie Abbott?"

Jones nodded vigorously and filled her mouth with food before she answered. It seemed to be her normal habit. "Yes, we've got her. Managed to keep her in a bit longer, lied to her parents, told them she'd got a temperature. He's a right bounder, that father. I reckon he hits that kid. Broken leg, broken arm, bashed on the head, fractured ribs; the story is that one of her fractures happened in the playground of a nursery school. Well, so it might have."

"What about the social worker?" asked Carmichael, mildly interested. At St. Jude's, her last job had been Staff Nurse on the children's ward, night duty, and she'd hated it, hated the ward, and in the end had hated the hospital, but she'd managed to put things right there. She sat a little straighter.

"Oh, they've been visited, much to old Abbott's disgust. Don't think he'll have them in the house any more. He's that kind of man, you know. I bet he could be violent."

"I met him; he came to the clinic last night to see Dr. Stephenson."

Jones nodded. "Oh, yes, I forgot. I thought you might have gone off duty, but you saw him, did you? What did you think of him?"

"A thoroughly objectionable little man," Carmichael said with vigour, and Jones nodded agreement.

"What did he say? Did you hear anything said, anything said in the clinic, I mean? I should have listened at the door; did you?"

Carmichael looked at Jones and then made a non-committal reply. "I don't know what was said, but when he came

out he was extremely rude to me, and I shan't forget it."
Carmichael's anger rose again at the thought of that man
saying to her, "Listening at the door; I thought Sisters were
far too dignified to do that kind of thing." She flushed, and
Jones finished her rice by scraping noisily with her fork and
popping the residue in her mouth. She laughed.

"You heard, did you? Well, you know as much as I do
then, but at least I did manage to get another few days off
for the kid. Poor little bugger. The trouble is with these
cases, the inquiries go on and on and nobody does enough
about it soon enough. I mean, look at . . ." Carmichael
was getting up.

"Aren't you having a sweet? It's apple crumble, not bad
with custard."

Carmichael shook her head. "No, I don't eat sweets, and
anyway I'm not particularly hungry. I'm going up to the
rest-room for coffee."

"O.K. I'll be up in a few minutes. I'll just have the apple
crumble. I know I shouldn't, but I will," said Jones, patting
the ample rise below the silver buckle of her black belt and
laughing again.

Carmichael left the canteen, collecting her coffee as she
went, and took it through into the Sisters' rest-room.

Even after three months, she was still conscious of her
rise to Sister from that of Staff Nurse, as she had been in her
last hospital. There were a great many differences and she
felt them with satisfaction.

The Sisters' rest-room had a television—not that one
used it, there was hardly time—but it was there. The chairs
were more comfortable than those in the ordinary staff
room, the decor more tasteful. There were fewer Sisters, of
course, than Staff Nurses and junior nurses, who were all
mixed in the same rest-room; therefore more could be
spent on a Sisters' retreat than the rest of the staff. It was
. . . satisfactory.

Carmichael put her coffee down on one of the small tables, sat down in one of the comfortable chairs, and opened her *Surgery for Nurses* again. But she was not reading with her usual concentration. She was thinking of Major Abbott and his cutting remark last night. Carmichael didn't like cutting remarks to go by her without some kind of retaliation. She liked to feel that she had, well, repaid . . . and she wondered what she could do to Major Abbott that would take him down a peg or two. Bashing his child? She wondered if he was. Could be. Well, she'd think about it, but on the whole she didn't think she'd let the incident pass. No, something should be done about it; something would come up, it always did. She half wished that Jones would hurry up and come and speak to her. She quite liked the fat, easygoing children's ward Sister, and it was after all getting a little lonely.

As Sister, she felt it necessary to keep a gap between herself and her Staff Nurses. Oh no, she wasn't going to fall into the trap of getting too familiar; other Sisters might— they even let the nurses call them by their Christian names. Not Carmichael. Carmichael was after more promotion, and after all, if you got right up the ladder to, say, Senior Nursing Officer, even higher, you couldn't have people calling you by your Christian name. No, she shook her head, and as she was shaking it, in walked Jones and noted the gesture.

"Something you don't agree with in the book? There's a hell of a lot I don't agree with that goes on in medicine," she said. "Appointing anyone like old Stephenson for instance."

"Stephenson?" Carmichael looked up, frowning. "Oh, you mean the paediatrician. Why, what's the matter with him?"

"Weak as water. He hasn't been here long, about nine months. We had one, Braithwaite; now there was a man.

He'd have settled with old Abbott, he wouldn't have had that kid go home, but Stephenson, well, he's new, you see, wouldn't want to put a foot wrong."

"That's very stupid, you've got to start as you mean to go on," said Carmichael, crisply, and Jones looked at her quizzically, putting her coffee down beside Carmichael's.

"And you've done that, have you?" she said, grinning.

"Most certainly I have," answered Carmichael. "Most certainly."

7

Miss Grant, the social worker allotted to the Marie Abbott case, drew her car into the kerb by the Abbotts' house. Surbiton Grove; somehow the name gave a picture of the surroundings. It was a select road, with houses that made Miss Grant dub it Stockbroker-Tudor dotted at discreet intervals along the road. A gravel drive led to each one, and the grass each side was neatly cut. A pretentious road, but speaking of people with very good incomes.

Miss Grant looked at the notes which she had taken from her briefcase. Major Abbott; the letters after his name showed him to be an accountant. Well, that type of profession fitted in with the kind of houses in the road.

Miss Grant got out of her car and locked it, then glanced back along the road to the house next door, which had outside a For Sale notice and an estate agent's paper banner with the word "Sold" stuck across it. She looked up at the vacant windows. The house had belonged to a Mrs. Wellstead, who had reported hearing Marie screaming during the night, and sometimes during the day; that had been her house, but she had moved. A junior social worker had been sent along to make some inquiries at the Abbotts' after this report, but to little avail; she had not been allowed in. Now Marie Abbott was in hospital for the second time.

Miss Grant walked the short distance between Braemar and the Abbotts' house, which was called, tritely enough, The Laburnums, and one laburnum tree bore out the name, standing at the foot of the drive. There were no gates to the houses; the grass stretched smoothly down to the row of shrubs which divided all the houses in the row from the road and pathway.

Miss Grant walked up the drive to the front door and looked at it appraisingly. It was made of wood, with simulated knots and graining. The top half was divided into six panels with bull's-eye glass. Below was a knocker, obviously not for use, for at the side hung a cast-iron black bell-pull which Miss Grant now used. She heard the bell in the house respond to her pull; that was all. She waited; no one came to the door. She stepped back and noticed that one bedroom window was open; the rest of the windows in the front of the house were closed. She rang again with the same result. The garage, beside the house, was closed, but Miss Grant guessed that Mr. Abbott, or Major Abbott, would be at work. Marie was in hospital and maybe Mrs. Abbott was out shopping. But, somehow, with that open window, she wondered. However, it was no use her going on ringing the bell. As a social worker, she knew this situation, and she knew that if Mrs. Abbott was there, if she didn't want to open the door, she wouldn't. On the other hand, she might be out.

Miss Grant made her way down the path and walked up to the entrance of another house, Holly Oaks, and into the drive. Each garden seemed to bear some similarity to its neighbours, but this was slightly more ambitious as to flowers. She rang the ordinary electric doorbell, and after a short pause the door was opened by a pleasant-looking middle-aged woman, who said, "Yes, what can I do for you?"

"Actually, I was calling to see Mrs. Abbott, and I wondered whether you knew if she was in or out. The bedroom window is open, and I just wondered, could she be asleep?"

"I really don't know, I don't think I can help you. She has

a car of her own, but when her husband is out, it's usually kept in the garage."

Miss Grant got the impression that the woman did not wish to become involved. Again, that was a situation that she was used to. "I see, well, the garage door is closed, so I can't really tell. Of course, Major Abbott will be at his office, I expect?"

The woman nodded and put her hand up and touched the immaculately waved and slightly silvered hair. "Yes, he may well be. Can I take any message?"

"Not really, it was just that I wanted to make some inquiries about her little daughter, Marie; she's in hospital, you know."

"Yes, I know." The woman clammed up more than ever.

"Poor little thing, she does seem to have a lot of accidents, doesn't she?" Miss Grant was fishing, but she caught nothing.

"Does she, indeed? I really wouldn't know. I believe Mrs. Abbott did tell me that she'd been in hospital before, she had a broken arm, or something." The woman was already backing and making to close the door on Miss Grant.

"Well, thank you for your help," said Miss Grant. "I'll have to call again sometime, perhaps the evening would be better, or do they have a daily woman?"

"Yes, yes, they do, they have the same one as I do, we share her, every other day. She should be there this morning, but she is a little deaf, maybe she didn't hear the bell."

"Oh, I see, thank you, that is a help. I'll go back and try again then." Miss Grant had scarcely got this remark out when the woman, slightly less agreeable than she had been when she first opened the door, nodded, and closed it firmly, but without rudeness. Miss Grant turned to go.

She walked again up the Abbotts' path, and this time rang the bell long and hard. After a time she heard a shuffling inside, then the door was flung back rather than opened. A thin, irritable-looking woman, who obviously had a bad head cold, greeted her. "Yes?"

Miss Grant repeated her formula, but this time loudly. "I'm Miss Grant, social worker. I've just come to see Mrs. Abbott. Is that possible?"

"She's out. Sorry," said the cleaning woman, using the duster in her hand to push the door again, but Miss Grant was determined.

"May I come in? I just want to ask . . ."

"Well, I . . ."

It was obvious the woman was fighting between a wish to hear what Miss Grant had to say and a dislike of letting her into the house, but curiosity won.

"Come in then, but don't make a noise," she said.

"Why? Is there another child in the house asleep?" asked Miss Grant.

The woman shook her head irritably. "No, I'm sorry, I didn't mean that, I was thinking Marie was still here." It was an obvious lie. "I'm Mrs. Danby. I just do for Mrs. Abbott and the lady next door. I come here every other day. What is it you want?"

"It's just that I was asking after Marie. I haven't been to the hospital today, and I thought Mrs. Abbott would probably have rung up, and as I was passing . . . Mrs. Abbott must be very worried about Marie; she seems to have so many accidents, doesn't she?"

Mrs. Danby had gone through into the kitchen, and Miss Grant had followed her. She stood, not offering Miss Grant a seat, with her back to the sink, the duster still in her hand. She looked straight at Miss Grant, her lips compressed into a thin line, her face closed. "I really wouldn't know, it's not for me to say, it's not for me to talk about, it's nothing to do with me." It was said so quickly, and with such determination, that Miss Grant knew that this would not be a source of information about the child.

"Well, perhaps you could tell me when Mrs. Abbott will be in, and I'll call back. And Major Abbott, does he come back for lunch?" She looked at her watch; it was twenty past twelve.

"Yes . . . No . . . Well, he sometimes does, you never know," said Mrs. Danby; again this hasty, quick, almost . . . was it fearful, or was it just hostile, manner? Miss Grant found it hard to assess.

"Well, it's nearly half past twelve. My time's finished, so I'd better get off," said Mrs. Danby, and she walked across the kitchen, took a light coat and a shopping bag from the hook on the back of the door, and repeated, "I must go, half past twelve is my time, and I'm going now. I'd better see you out."

"Well, thank you for being so helpful," said Miss Grant without a trace of sarcasm in her voice, for in a way Mrs. Danby had been helpful, and as the cleaning woman slipped on her coat Miss Grant took an appraising look round the kitchen. Washing machine, tumble dryer, Kenwood mixer, beautifully fitted cupboard, split-level cooker, everything speaking of money, neat, very clean. Well, of course, Mrs. Danby had just spent the morning there. As they walked through the hall, too, Miss Grant took in everything; it was her job to do so. A large plant, the name of which she didn't know, stood in the corner, the leaves shining. The parquet floor, too, was beautifully kept, and the two rugs lying criss-cross over it were obviously expensive. The table, and the rest of the furniture in the hall, were beautifully polished.

"You certainly keep the house immaculately, Mrs. Danby, one would hardly know there was a child here, there's usually a toy or something." She turned and smiled at Mrs. Danby but got little response.

"Oh, Marie has to keep her things tidy, she has a room of her own, Mrs. Abbott doesn't like things lying about." At that moment there was a slight noise, and both Miss Grant and Mrs. Danby automatically turned their heads towards the stairs.

"Is there someone upstairs?" asked Miss Grant.

"There's nobody up there." Mrs. Danby moved a little more quickly, pushing Miss Grant in front of her, and opened the front door. As she did so, a very lean cat walked in.

Miss Grant was surprised. "Is that Mrs. Abbott's cat?" she asked.

Mrs. Danby nodded. "It's Marie's," she said.

"It's very thin," said Miss Grant, looking after it as it went towards the kitchen. She loved cats. "Has it got some food in there?" she asked.

"I'm sure I don't know, it's nothing to do with me," said Mrs. Danby, and they both watched the cat walk into the kitchen.

At that moment there was suddenly a voice speaking from outside the front door. "No, indeed, it's nothing to do with Mrs. Danby, or you, whoever you are." It was Major Abbott. His car was parked at the bottom of the drive, and that was why they had not heard him drive up to the house.

"Oh, er . . . sorry, sir. This is Miss er-um—a social worker. She came to ask about Marie, to see if Mrs. Abbott had heard anything this morning, but I told her Mrs. Abbott was out." The straight gaze that passed between Mrs. Danby and Major Abbott was not lost on Miss Grant.

"Well, Major Abbott," said Miss Grant, "Mrs. Danby was very kind and let me come in and ask. I understand Mrs. Abbott is out, perhaps she's gone to the hospital and is already with Marie."

"Is that all, Mrs. Danby? Have you finished?" Major Abbott ignored Miss Grant and spoke directly to his cleaning woman.

"Yes, sir, I'm off now, I've done everything. I've . . .

The . . ." It was obvious that Mrs. Danby was embarrassed and didn't know quite how to handle this situation and was feeling a little upset at Major Abbott's attitude to the fact that she had let Miss Grant into the house.

"Very well, I understand, it's quite all right, off you go. I'll see you the day after tomorrow, right?" Mrs. Danby nodded and slid past him sideways; he remained standing in the doorway. Miss Grant was trapped, she could hardly push past him, indeed she didn't want to. An interview with Major Abbott was better than nothing, so she backed a little into the hall and said, "Perhaps I may have a word with you, Major Abbott."

"If you wish, but I can't think what it's about." He strode ahead of her into what she took to be the sitting-room. He did not ask her to sit down, but turned round abruptly. "Well, what is it, why have you come here, what do you want to know?"

"It's just that we're a little worried about Marie, your little daughter, she does seem to be so very accident-prone."

"Oh, you're another snooper, are you? I suppose it's because of that bloody Mrs. Wellstead next door. Thank God she's moved. She reported that she heard Marie screaming, didn't she. Is that it?" Major Abbott put his hand up and smoothed his moustache, both sides, over his top lip, but his face had two high spots of pink on each cheek bone. Before Miss Grant could answer, he went on: "I don't know what this kind of visit insinuates. That we beat the child, is that it, cruelly treat her? Well, let me tell you that I'm not going to put up with any more visits like this. I believe you came before, but that my wife didn't let you in, is that right?"

Miss Grant nodded. "Major Abbott," she said determinedly, before he could speak again. "This is only to inquire if Marie has received any treatment that has caused her to have these injuries. We are not insinuating anything. She may be being bullied at school. She goes to a nursery school, does she not? It can happen, you know, and on both admissions her body was rather bruised. Little children can be very nasty to each other, even small ones. It has to be looked into, and this time . . ."

"Well, as you know, she did break her arm in the school playground, but if there was any bullying, I'd know about it, and so would her mother, I think." Major Abbott paused; he was slightly mollified, it seemed. Miss Grant was perhaps not insinuating quite what he thought. "No, I'm quite certain the school is all right, and that Marie is just one of those children who fall about—children do, don't they?"

Miss Grant nodded. "Yes indeed, they do, but Marie just seems to fall about more than most, and this has caused some worry at the hospital. That is why I called."

"Well, the matter's cleared up then, isn't it? You've seen me, and that Marie has a good home." He looked complacently round the sitting-room. "I imagine that you have come to the conclusion that this is not the kind of home where parents live who would beat up a child, am I right?"

"The kind of home doesn't always come into it, Major Abbott, but certainly you have a beautifully kept house." She looked round the sitting-room. The comfortable overstuffed furniture was new, modern, expensive; across the room was a drinks cart, loaded with bottles, with brass rails, beautifully polished, and glasses shining. The fireplace too, full of logs, with a gas poker sticking into it; the ornaments dotted round the room to Miss Grant's practised eye were good and unpretentious. The whole room shone with cleanliness, not a thread or mark on the carpet.

"Yes indeed. Could I see Marie's room? Mrs. Danby said she had a special room to herself. No jammy fingers on the furniture down here." Miss Grant tried to make the conversation light.

"No indeed, we don't allow that sort of thing, my wife is very house-proud and so am I."

"Marie is kept out of these rooms, then?"

This last sentence finished Major Abbott's small reserve of patience. "Get out," he said. "You're insinuating that we keep her locked up upstairs, is that it? Well, we don't, so please go, and if I have any more intrusions, or insinuations like this, I shall sue, do you understand?"

Miss Grant knew the signs. She had come to the end of his tolerance, and she would have to go, but she had learned a lot for her report. She walked towards the door, and at that moment a wail came from the kitchen.

"The cat?" said Miss Grant mildly.

"I know that, it's Marie's cat, a damn nuisance," said Major Abbott. "And even the cat, Miss Grant, has nothing to do with you. Now, do you mind?" He walked ahead of her and opened the front door. She walked past him, and as she did so, she looked him directly in the eyes. "Thank you, Major Abbott, you've been a great help," she said. Major Abbott slammed the door behind her.

Miss Grant walked down the drive, unlocked and got into her car, threw the briefcase she was carrying on to the back seat, and sat for a moment, her hands beating gently on the wheel, thinking, memorizing. Yes, she would have quite a lot to put into her report; that beautifully kept house—it didn't seem possible that a child lived there at all. She tried to imagine a three-year-old running up and down those stairs, or over the polished parquet floor in the hall, or playing in the garden. There was the cat, at least they allowed her to have a pet, but even that . . . She shook her head a little, put the keys in the ignition, started up the car, and backed away from the large Rover parked outside the Abbotts' house, skirted it, and drove away. The report she was going to make, should it become necessary to send it to a preliminary case conference, was already forming in her mind.

8

The weekend was looked forward to in varying degrees by the hospital personnel of St. Matthew's.

Those who worked the five-day week, Monday to Friday, looked forward to it, and Friday evening was reached by the laboratory technicians, office staff, by the theatre staff and the doctors, except those on call, with relief. To the wards it made little or no difference; they were manned almost to the same degree as they were during the week.

The Casualty department looked forward to the weekend with mixed feelings, according to what functions or sporting occasions were taking place in or around the town of Dwyford, which the hospital served. A cycling rally or a motor-bike scramble would mean more staff on duty to deal with a pile-up, if one happened, and young men brought in with grazed thighs, broken ribs.

To Carmichael, who came under the five-day heading, it was pure bliss.

She woke on the Saturday morning, and immediately was filled with a sense of security and appreciation of what she still looked on as her new flat, though she'd been in it nearly three months. She had been lucky, very lucky, to get it. The fact that the famous Holly had had to vacate it to go to another job had been a stroke of luck, and Carmichael, frugal with her money in her last post, had saved and saved towards the day when she would be a Sister. And here she was now with the dreamed-of flat and the dreamed-of car. True, it was only a small flat, and the car only a Mini, but brand-new and shining. Carmichael thought of it now, sitting in the garage in the courtyard below, safely locked up. She loved that little car. She had passed her test ready for it ages ago, and kept up her licence, waiting; Carmichael was quite good at that.

She lay in bed, looking round the room. Her hay fever had momentarily disappeared; she knew it would be back the moment she went out, but at the moment that didn't matter. She must get up and make herself a cup of tea. She looked at the clock on her bedside table—twenty past eight —she had slept well. Carmichael was not normally a good sleeper.

She put her hands behind her head for a moment's more rest—marvellous—and gazed out of the window on to the sunny morning. Her flat was three flights up, with no lift, but what did that matter? When you got there, even the corridor was beautifully kept. She remembered her last bed-sitting-room, with its scratched door, remembered the corridor, with the furtive hands coming out to grab the morning paper or a bottle of milk, and sometimes someone shuffling along the passage in an old plaid dressing gown and carpet slippers. Nothing like that here; this, though small, was quite a decent flat in quite a decent building. It looked out on to a square of garden, which, of course, Carmichael couldn't see; lying in bed, she only saw the intense blue sky. Another sunny day.

She got out of bed, thrust her feet into slippers, put on her dressing-gown, and padded into the tiny kitchen. She switched on the electric kettle—all her own—everything bought with the money that had been so worth saving. True, the carpets and curtains had come with the flat. Holly, whom she had never met, had sold her those; she'd sent her a cheque. That had been great, because the extra expense of new carpeting and curtains would have made the whole thing—well, she wouldn't have been able to do it.

Carmichael put her hand on the kettle to see if it was heating; it should do, brand-new. At that moment the kettle began to sing comfortably. She withdrew her hand, went over and picked up a small, pretty tin, a legacy from her bed-sitting-room. She had, of course, brought the nicest things with her. She opened the tin, took out a tea-bag, put the tin back in place, moved it slightly because it wasn't quite symmetrical with the tin of sugar and the tin of flour, on top of the small refrigerator.

While she was waiting for the kettle to boil, she automatically wiped down the working area with a damp cloth. It hardly needed it, but Carmichael was fastidious. When she had done this, wrung out the cloth, shaken it and hung it up, the kettle clicked off. She warmed the teapot, and popped in the tea-bag, poured in the boiling water, put the lid on the teapot, and covered it with a tea-cosy.

She put the teapot on the tray, already laid the night before; a pretty teacup and saucer, teaspoon, a little bowl of sugar, and milk jug; the china of course matched. She poured milk into the jug from the bottle taken from the refrigerator, and as she did so, she stood back a little and looked at the tray. It reminded her . . . the face of an old colleague flashed before her: Marion Hughes. She remembered her tea-tray with the blue flowered china. Well, Marion Hughes wouldn't be using that tea-tray any more. Carmichael smirked at the tray and carried it through to the bedroom, and put it on the bedside table; then she walked into the tiny lobby which served as a hall to her flat and took the *Daily Mail* from her letter-box, and with her paper went back into her bedroom and slipped into bed—luxury. She flicked through the paper, poured herself a cup of tea, added sugar, stirred it, and drank. Saturday morning—bliss.

She opened the drawer of the bedside table and got out a small notebook and pen and began to jot down the things she had to get this morning—the weekend shopping. She thought she'd have . . . the list was small, but adequate. Vegetables, meat, a bottle of lemonade; should she get a bottle of sherry and ask someone round, like Sister Jones, should she? She added sherry to the list, then shook her head. Not yet, she wasn't ready for that yet, she was quite self-sufficient; the flat, car, that was enough, she didn't want anybody, and why should she spend money on sherry? She didn't like it. No, she crossed the word "sherry" out, put the pen back in the drawer, threw the list to the bottom of the bed, got up again, went through to the equally tiny bathroom, and ran herself a bath.

There was no doubt about it, Saturday morning was perfect, too perfect perhaps to go to the shops. Carmichael decided to dust the car, tidy the garage, and do a wee bit of housework. She could go out this afternoon; it wouldn't be so crowded. She nodded to herself in satisfaction and then found, with annoyance, that she had to blow her nose; it was getting stuffed up already. Still, it didn't matter here, it didn't matter what she looked like. Here, she was herself, Carmichael.

She went through into the bathroom, turned off the taps, took off her dressing-gown and night-dress, slipped into the steaming bath, and lay back. It was wonderful being a Sister.

9

Sister Jones on the children's ward was reacting bitterly to the Abbotts, far more bitterly than perhaps she should professionally; but Dr. Stephenson didn't come in on Saturdays, and here they were determined to brook no more delays. They were taking Marie home, and that was that. They walked into the ward with determination, Mrs. Abbott following behind her husband, who looked decidedly dangerous.

Jones knew there was nothing she could do; she had to let the child go. She'd managed to keep her a few more days, but she was going to note the reaction of the child when she saw her parents were going to take her home, that was for sure.

"She's in the cubicle. As she ran that temperature we decided to keep her away from the other children, but she seems all right now." She looked suspiciously at Mrs. Abbott, a brittle, rather fragile-looking woman, who looked round the ward with quick, darting glances, taking everything in, Jones felt, herself in particular.

"Well, we've brought her things." Major Abbott indicated the suitcase his wife was carrying. "We've bought her a new frock—perhaps that'll please her. It'll make people think we treat her kindly, eh?" He looked at Sister Jones. It was a direct challenge, a challenge that the Sister did not dare take up.

"She's down here, in the last cubicle," she said, and walked forward, the parents following her. She opened one glass door for them, and then the second, and they trooped through. She watched the child. They had come in quietly and Marie was playing with some plastic skittles. She had other things on the bed, but the skittles seemed to be occupying her. She was banging one lightly on the other, head bent forward, her fair hair screening her face. She looked up suddenly and saw Sister. A half-smile came on her face, then she noticed her parents were there as well, and the child seemed to freeze. Was it fear, or just surprise? Jones stared at the child.

"Hallo, Marie darling, how are you, my sweet?" said Mrs. Abbott. Sister Jones automatically let down the side of the cot, and Marie's mother came up to the child, knelt down beside the cot, and attempted to take Marie in her arms. Marie leant away, looking at her father, those big blue eyes very round now. Then she suddenly put her arms round her mother's neck and held her tightly. Her mother picked her out of the cot.

"Well, come on, get her dressed, I'll wait outside," said Major Abbott abruptly. He had not addressed the child at all, and turning, he went out of the two doors, beckoning Sister to follow him. She did so.

"Now look, Sister," he said, and his voice was threatening.

"If you wish to speak to me, I would suggest you come to my office." Sister Jones walked, with her rather waddling walk, away from him, went into her office, sat down at her desk, and motioned to him to sit in the chair beside it. "Yes, you wish to say something to me?" she asked.

"I do. I know you've kept this child in on some pretext or other, but now she's going home, and I want you to know this, that I'm withdrawing her utterly from Dr. Stephenson and this hospital's care. I think he's useless; he says there are tests to be carried out, well, they will be carried out. If she's got this . . . disease that he suggests that may make her bones more fragile, then it will be dealt with, but I wish to have nothing more to do with him. Is that understood?"

"If you wish me to convey such a message, I'm afraid it is quite impossible, Major Abbott. You must write to him yourself. You're taking this child home against his wishes, and I'm afraid you have to sign this form." She pushed it towards him.

He read it, and signed it without demur. "Yes, I'm quite happy to do that, anything to get her out of here, and away from these vile insinuations that have been made against me," he said.

"Vile insinuations?" Sister Jones looked at him.

"Oh yes, I know what you're all insinuating, you're insinuating that this child is badly treated at home. Well, I could sue you for that, you know." He glared at Sister Jones.

"Thank you," said Jones as she took the form from him and put it in the drawer at the side of her desk. "As I was saying, anything you wish to say must be said to Dr. Stephenson. If you wish to write or see him again, that is entirely up to you." Abbott nodded as Jones and he rose and walked out of the office.

At that moment Mrs. Abbott walked up the ward, holding Marie by the hand. Abbott motioned with his head for his wife to follow him. As Marie's mother passed her, Jones caught a distinct whiff of whisky—at ten o'clock in the morning! Jones determined to mention it to Dr. Stephenson.

They walked out of the ward, Marie clutching a small Teddy bear that her mother had evidently brought with her in the suitcase. The child turned round as she got to the door, and looked at Sister Jones, but Mrs. Abbott made no effort to let the child say goodbye. She pushed open the swing-doors of the ward and pushed the child through, but even as she did so Marie hadn't withdrawn her eyes from Sister Jones' face, but continued looking over her shoulder at her until the doors swung to and hid the child from view. Jones felt that last look had been pleading.

"Damn, blast, bugger, and shit," said Jones under her breath. "I don't trust that pair at all. How the hell could Dr. Stephenson let her . . . Well, I'll ring him up and tell him the kid's gone home. I damn well will, disturbing his weekend or not." She went back into her office, pulled the phone towards her, dialled the telephone exchange and asked for Dr. Stephenson's number.

10

Carmichael had cleaned and polished the already cleaned and polished flat, she'd Hoovered the carpet on which there was hardly ever a speck of dust, and generally "tidied up," as she put it. Then she prepared to do the most enjoyable thing she found to do every weekend—dust the car. She used it every day to go to work, but at weekends it somehow seemed more special that it should be bright and shining.

She went downstairs, unlocked the garage and threw the door up, and looked with smug satisfaction at the rear end of the Mini. There was a slight smudge of mud on the yellow number-plates; she must do something about that. She got into the car and backed it out into the sunlight, then went upstairs and fetched a cloth and a bucket with a little water in the bottom. The car didn't need washing, but she must get that mud off. She took also a soft yellow duster, specially kept for the Mini. She carefully removed the speck of mud from the back number-plate, and was busy gently dusting the top of the car when one of her neighbours came down and threw open his garage door. "You be careful you don't polish that car right away and make it disappear," he said, laughing. He was an elderly man. Carmichael had met him before; they were just on speaking terms. Carmichael smiled her downward smile but said nothing.

"You can have a go at mine any time," said the man,

walking into his garage, where a rather dusty, dirty old Princess stood.

Carmichael felt she must say something. "I've got quite enough with mine, thank you." Her voice was prim and the man walked over and looked at the car.

"It looks really smart, that Mini, really smart. You bought it new though, didn't you?" Carmichael nodded.

"M-m. Well, I say buy British cars, and you seem pleased enough with yours."

"I love it." Carmichael spoke half to him and half to herself. She put her hand on the sun-warmed bonnet of the car caressingly. It was true, she did love it, more than anything in her life. Her neighbour smiled, walked away, got into his own car, backed it out, and went off down the small drive that led past their block of flats.

It was pleasant there in the sunshine. Carmichael went upstairs again to fetch her shopping bag and her shopping list. She looked at her watch: half past two. Just right—the shops wouldn't be too full again yet, and anyway most people seemed to do the bulk of their shopping in the morning. She usually went out in the afternoon to do hers. Suddenly, she thought she'd spoil herself and have a chicken; after all, it always came in cold and with salad. She took out a pencil and added it to her shopping list, and popped the list into her bag. She went downstairs again to her garage after latching the front door of her flat behind her.

Carmichael got into the Mini, which still had that delightful smell that new cars have, its seats still covered with the cellophane cover that Carmichael felt she would never take off. There was a slight film of dust on the top part of the steering wheel, and Carmichael took the yellow duster that she had put into the glove compartment and dusted the wheel off. She belted up, backed the car a little further to make turning easier, and drove out into the road. She

looked searchingly both ways. Carmichael was a very careful driver; she couldn't bear the thought of the Mini being
bumped or damaged in any way. This made her drive even
more carefully, more for the car's sake than her own.

It was a short way to the town, and it was only the pleasure of driving the car that made Carmichael take it at all.
She could, as she had done when she was working at St.
Jude's, have carried the shopping back, no matter how
heavy. But now, after all, she had a car, and she was a Sister.
These things, they were enjoyable in themselves. She
smiled complacently, then took a tissue from out of a
packet, also in the front compartment of the car, and blew
her nose. Her hay fever wasn't getting any better, but still
the weekend lay ahead, and even hay fever couldn't dull
that pleasure. She drove first to the greengrocer's and
bought her vegetables for the week, then she drove to the
main street to the butcher's, looking carefully for a parking
space. At this time in the afternoon it was easier to find one
than in the morning, and there, outside the estate agent's,
she saw a space.

Carmichael drove carefully towards it, signalling that she
was going to the right of the road, parked the car with a
good three-foot space in front of her, where stood a Rover.
She looked at it critically, got out of the car, locked it, and
went forward to see if the Rover had enough room to get
out. Yes, there was a good three yards before the next car
was parked in front of the Rover. That was important; Carmichael thought of these things. After all, if a car in front of
you backed, and she wasn't there . . . No, there was loads
of room. She looked at the Mini again; it shone in the
sunlight. She glanced inside to see that the brake was on.
Yes. She put the keys carefully in her handbag and went
across to the butcher's.

After a few minutes Carmichael came back with her pur-
chase, unlocked the car, got in, and sat for a moment before

she put on her safety-belt, thinking. She snapped open her bag, took out the list, and checked. Yes, that was everything. She put the shopping bag on the seat beside her, popped the list inside to get it out of the way, snapped the clasp of her handbag, having taken out the car keys, and put it in front of her shopping bag.

The key in the ignition, she was about to start the engine when she saw Major Abbott. He was walking out of the estate agent's holding some keys in his hand, followed closely by a woman who she presumed must be Mrs. Abbott. Her anger rose again at the sight of him. Beastly man, I hope he doesn't see me, she thought, but he gave no glance in her direction, merely nodded at something his wife said, opened the door of the car in front, and got in. His wife went round to the other side and stood waiting for him to unlock the door for her. He took his time; he would, she thought.

Meek, I should think, thought Carmichael to herself, if that is Mrs. Abbott. Yet she hadn't looked meek exactly; she looked a bit vixenish. Who wouldn't, married to him? She watched them curiously, wondering what he was doing in the estate agent's. Buying a house, she supposed. Well, Carmichael's mind registered it but was going to do no more about it, until something happened which changed the whole course of Abbott's life, what there was left of it.

Carmichael didn't attempt to start her car; she was going to wait until the Rover had driven away. She saw him turn and say something impatiently to his wife. She turned to him, looking equally angry, and said something back. The engine of the Rover started up, and Carmichael expected it to draw away. It did, but only slightly, turning its front wheels as it did so. Carmichael then noticed that the car in front was a different one from the one she had so carefully checked; it was closer to the Rover. Abbott got into reverse gear and backed the car to give himself a little more turning space to avoid the car in front, and Carmichael felt a jolt as he hit her offside headlamp. There was a tinkle of glass, then the Rover was gone.

Carmichael got out of her car, her heart racing; her knees felt weak. She went round to the front and looked.

"Pranged you there, did you get his number?" a passer-by said.

Carmichael looked at him; her face was ashen.

"It's only the lamp, not much damage."

"Enough," said Carmichael. She got back into the car while the man kicked the glass from the lamp into the gutter.

"Careful now," he called, but Carmichael was beyond being careful. She turned out into the main stream of traffic, and then she saw the Rover again. It had only reached the bottom of the main street, where the traffic-lights were holding it up. Abbott had made no attempt to stop and inquire what damage he had done; perhaps he didn't even know he'd done it, but he was going to. Carmichael stood waiting behind two more cars; the traffic-lights changed and she watched the Rover turn left. She switched on her signal, got into the left lane and found there was nothing between her and the Rover—the other two cars were turning right. Her fury mounted. The injury to the thing she loved most in the world made her feel sick, a feeling she recognized; she had had it before.

She cautiously turned left, following the Rover out of the town along a country road, then suddenly it turned into the driveway of a house standing almost alone. There was a For Sale notice stuck outside the large gates. Carmichael realized she had been right as to why he had been in the estate agent's. She drew her car into the side of the road, and in the shadow of the hedge that screened the house and drive from the road, stopped her engine and got out but didn't lock the damaged car. She walked forward and again turned and looked at the smashed lamp. She felt that she, herself, had been delivered a physical blow. She hurt for the car; it was a strange feeling. She felt her pulse still racing, put her hands up and held her face for a moment. Her cheeks felt hot, and yet the face reflected in the chromium of the side mirror of the car looked pale.

Without a thought in her head she walked the short distance along the hedge and peered round the drive of the house. She noticed the name on the open gate: Millstream House. Carmichael looked up the drive, and there was the Rover, parked in front of the house. Mr. and Mrs. Abbott were disappearing inside. There was a man waiting on the steps to meet them. He was obviously the owner of the red car in front of the Rover. They disappeared inside the house, and Carmichael stood, her mind still curiously blank. A vague feeling that something was going to happen was trying to fill the blankness, but she couldn't think what, so she waited.

Ten minutes must have gone by, more; Carmichael had no feeling about the time. She stood watching, out of sight, watching. She was still conscious of a trembling, a feeling of weakness. Suddenly she saw Abbott, Mrs. Abbott, and the man come out of the house and stand on the steps, chatting. Major Abbott took something out of his pocket; Carmichael, drawing back into the hedge, saw it was a pipe. He came down the steps, passing between the two cars, across the drive, and as he did so, he called back to his wife. "You go and have another look round, dear, with Mr. Jensen. I've quite decided, but I don't want to make your mind up for you. Go back and have another look round, and think about it. I'm going to have a smoke, I've made up my mind." Mrs. Abbott nodded, and the two went back into the house.

Major Abbott crossed the grass and started to walk down a slope, out of Carmichael's range of vision. She crossed quickly behind the gates; this gave her a better view. She could even walk a little way inside the gates without him seeing her. She did so and stood behind a large rhododendron bush, watching; Abbott was filling his pipe, and she watched him light it and puff contentedly, and throw the match away into the stream that bubbled at the bottom of the garden. She turned a little further and saw why the house had its name; there was a water-mill. She peered round further and saw that up the hill away from the water-mill was another house; presumably the water-mill was owned . . . Vaguely there came to her mind that there was a place along this road where you could buy granary bread, that was why . . . Her mind was beginning to function again. She watched the wheel, she could just see the top of it, turning slowly, and she listened to the rush of water. She was fascinated.

Abbott must have found it so, too, for he stood gazing down for some minutes, then turned and looked towards the house, walked a few more paces along, nearer the wheel, but still looking at it reflectively.

Carmichael suddenly came out from her hiding-place and approached him. It was some seconds before he caught sight of her, then his eyes rounded in surprise. He turned from the wheel and faced her. "Are you after the house, too, have you come to view it? I didn't know anyone else—" It was obvious that he didn't recognize her out of context. Carmichael shook her head, and suddenly recognition dawned on Major Abbott.

"Why, you're that Sister from the hospital, aren't you? The one—you were in—when I came to see . . ." Carmichael nodded, and twitched her head in that familiar way she had when she was highly nervous. She put her hand up to see that her bun wasn't springing hairs out of place.

Major Abbott looked at her, and in his eyes was that look she always saw in men's eyes, no appreciation of what she looked like, no appreciation of her as a woman, she knew.

She had seen it in the mirror—her pale, fawn face; pale, fawn hair. She daren't even sunbathe to make herself brown, because she burned, and there was no glory of honey colour that some of the other nurses achieved, just a red face and a skinning nose.

Abbott went on: "You're not after the house, are you?" His voice was disbelieving, and yet you could see that he wasn't sure. He was probably thinking, guessed Carmichael, After all, you don't know how much these women are worth.

She tried to keep a grimace from her face as she answered. "Oh no, Major Abbott, I'm not after the house." She came closer to him. "You are, though. Do you like it, does your wife like it?"

It was obvious that Major Abbott was thrown off balance by this type of approach. He didn't know why she was here; he couldn't quite think how to handle the situation. He took a step back. "Yes, my wife's looking it over again, I think we'll have it. I've decided I like it, ideal place for the child." Did he throw that in for good measure? After all, it was the only connection he had with this unattractive woman.

Carmichael nodded. "Yes, a very nice place for Marie—it is Marie, isn't it?" He nodded. "Aren't you a little afraid of the river though, of her having an accident of some kind?"

"What the hell do you mean by that?" Abbott's face hardened.

Carmichael went closer and looked him full in the eyes. "Just what I said, Major Abbott. After all, a country place like this, a stream, lots of trees; children are apt to climb trees, aren't they, and fall out of them and break something, you never know, drown even."

Abbott took another step back as Carmichael drew near him; but she came forward again. He tried to amend the violence of his last remark. "Oh, I see what you mean. Well, yes, there's always a risk with children; we shall have to take special care with the stream . . ."

"Yes indeed, a great risk with children, particularly with Marie, it seems."

"I don't know what you mean, or if you're insinuating anything, or if you're just a bloody fool, just a snooper—after all you were listening, weren't you, in that bloody clinic?"

Carmichael smiled her usual smile and nodded. "I was listening, and I think you can take it that I was insinuating something, couldn't you, Major Abbott?" she said, and again she stepped forward. Carmichael was not looking at him now, she was looking behind him, as she had suddenly foreseen what was going to happen. She knew what she would do.

Major Abbott was about to speak, his face reddening with rage. He put his hand to his collar as though it was too tight. "You bitch, you ugly bitch, I'll get you for this. I won't forget this, I'll report it to someone or other. I'll report you and Stephenson." He jammed the pipe back in his mouth. Carmichael took another step forward, and he took one step back, the one step she wanted. He was directly over the water-wheel. Carmichael put the flat of her hand in the middle of Major Abbott's chest and pushed.

"Hit and run. You smashed my car lamp," she said.

Abbott made nothing at all of the last words he ever heard. He hurtled backwards with hardly a sound, the pipe still clenched between his teeth; he landed neatly on the wheel.

Carmichael looked down at the still, spread-eagled form. She looked round at the house, but there was no sign of the estate agent or Mrs. Abbott; she turned back and watched. Major Abbott was quite still, he had fallen head first and must have stunned himself; the wheel went on turning and Major Abbott turned with it. His face looked pink as he went round and down between the mill-wheel and the wall. He disappeared. The wheel gave a little shudder and stopped. There was no sound, no sign of Major Abbott left. She glanced again at the house—still no sign of life. Carmichael stood where Major Abbott had stood, and looked down at the wheel. It looked exactly the same, except that it was no longer turning; the uppermost blades were wet, slightly green and slimy. Perhaps he had just gone into the water and would swim away, the cold water would bring him to. She wondered, but she didn't think there would be room. The wheel had stopped, come to a grinding halt; something had stopped it; she knew it was the body of Major Abbott.

Carmichael waited for a few more seconds, then she saw it, bobbing down the stream, between the man-made brick walls. It was his pipe, and to her great satisfaction it was followed by a thin stream of red. Carmichael watched, after another quick glance at the house, for a few more seconds. She was slightly worried about them coming out, but she knew in her heart that she would have plenty of time. She watched the stream of blood widen a little in the slightly turbulent water. That was that. She listened again; only water bubbled, no other sound.

She turned, walked down the drive, out of the gate, got into her injured car, closed the door quietly, and started up the engine.

As she passed the gate, she looked in and saw the front door of Millstream House opening. Carmichael slid the car into gear gently and drove away before Mrs. Abbott and the estate agent emerged.

A little further along the road she passed another sign, not For Sale this time but a notice which read Wholemeal Flour Bread, then a further sign underneath it: Brandon Mill Bread for Sale. She wondered idly when they would start grinding the flour again. Monday, no doubt, but perhaps someone would see the wheel wasn't turning before then. Well, no matter . . .

As Carmichael drove, she was conscious of the same surge of feeling coming into her as she had had that morning at St. Jude's, bringing confidence and relaxation, which only now seemed to have been receding a little. It was a wonderful sensation to get back, the feeling of omnipotence. Yes, that was a good word, for after all, ending a life like that, and she was sure she had ended it, yes, that was godlike, omnipotent, and she had done it to the right person.

With Carmichael around, there was no need to wait, no need for the Social Services to bungle their way through things, as they did, with their meetings and their discussions. No, Carmichael was there to settle such problems, and anyway, she needed to settle problems, they were meat and drink to her, she realized. She was the justice-bringer, she was the person who coped; others talked.

Major Abbott . . . A downward smile seemed stuck on her face as she drove her Mini. Even the child, about whom she cared little, her injuries were amply paid for; and even the injury to her beloved Mini seemed less terrible now; and anyway, he wouldn't do that kind of thing again.

Oh, she had learned something from Marion Hughes: she would keep a stern, strict eye on her nurses, that was not bad, but she would always try to be just; she wanted to be liked. Wherever Carmichael went, justice would follow. Gone for the moment was the doubt of her own powers; in the back of her mind the little, niggly wondering was gone. Yes, but for how long?

11

A few seconds after Carmichael's car had driven away, Mrs. Abbott and Mr. Jensen, the estate agent, came out of the front door of Millstream House. Mr. Jensen was talking animatedly, but Mrs. Abbott was silent.

"I'm so glad you like it, Mrs. Abbott; it really is a lovely property and so picturesque, I do hope you'll enjoy living here." He was voluble in his pleasure; it was an expensive property, and he was glad to be rid of it. He had shown many people round, but the price, in the end, had balked them. It didn't seem to matter too much to Major Abbott, who had, however, managed to beat him down a little. Still, the afternoon was getting on, and he had given up a round of golf to sell the house, but now he wanted to get away.

As Mrs. Abbott and he walked towards the two cars, he took his keys out of his pocket, and was twirling them in his hand. They both looked round for Major Abbott.

"Where can my husband have got to?" said Mrs. Abbott. "He must have walked outside, up the lane, I suppose, to see what it's like. I hope he won't be long."

"Oh no, I'm sure he won't." Then Jensen paused and looked at the two cars. "Oh, do you drive, Mrs. Abbott?" he asked. "I can't get my car out, you see, unless the Rover's moved. Perhaps you would like to back it out into the lane." Mrs. Abbott shook her head, and as she spoke, Jensen noticed again, as he had in the house, the smell of whisky on her breath.

"I never drive my husband's car, but I'm sure he won't be

long. Perhaps if the keys are in the car, you could back it out yourself, if you are in a hurry." She looked inside and shook her head; the keys were not hanging from the ignition. She walked to the gate and looked up and down, while behind her the estate agent clicked his tongue impatiently. Mrs. Abbott came back.

"Perhaps you wouldn't mind if I backed it out, I have driven a Rover before, I am quite safe with it." Mr. Jensen smiled amiably.

"Certainly, I've already said you could, but I've looked and the keys are not in the car, I'm afraid. That's not unusual, my husband always takes them out, in case someone . . ."

"Well, we'll just have to wait," Jensen said, trying to hide his impatience. "Perhaps he'll only be a few minutes."

Mrs. Abbott nodded, but she also seemed to be getting slightly agitated. "Stupid of him to go away like this and not tell us. I mean, I hope he hasn't gone too far up the road."

The estate agent looked at Mrs. Abbott and thought she looked strange and rather peculiar, and wondered just how much she had had to drink before they arrived at the house. "Perhaps he's gone to buy some of the granary bread."

"Granary bread!" Mrs. Abbott looked at him as if he were mad. "My husband would hardly go shopping for bread," she said coldly.

Mr. Jensen hastily amended the remark. "Oh, I didn't mean that, I meant he was probably looking at the house along the road, where they sell the bread and the flour, you know."

"I doubt it, my husband's not interested in that sort of thing. I'm sorry you're delayed, but that's just how it is, we shall have to wait for him, but I really think it is most inconsiderate." Mrs. Abbott finished the remark coldly.

"Do you mind if I smoke, Mrs. Abbott?" Mr. Jensen got out a packet of cigarettes and offered her one. Mrs. Abbott took one, and he noticed that her hands were shaking. He lighted first her cigarette, and then his own, the smoke filtering up in the sunlit air. Mrs. Abbott turned away, puffing nervously at her cigarette, and looked at the mill.

"Quite a feature, isn't it, and especially as it doesn't have to be kept up by the owner of Millstream House. You get all the joy out of the mill itself without any of the trouble." Mr. Jensen, an estate agent to the last, was still voluble, if irritable.

"Yes." Mrs. Abbott nodded abstractedly and then looked towards the gate again, then the other way to a small copse which lay a little way along the stream. There was no sign of Major Abbott.

"The wheel keeps turning, too—very slowly, of course, when the sluice gates are shut—but it's always turning, and I think that's quite a talking point, isn't it, for visitors, I mean." Mr. Jensen was copying Mrs. Abbott with the short, quick puffs he was taking on his cigarette; there was a tension building up.

He walked down the slope to the stream and looked at the wheel. "Oh, it's stopped," he said. "I've never seen that happen before, it's always been going when I . . ." His voice tailed off, and he looked harder at the water gushing out from under the wheel. Mrs. Abbott watched him and then sensed the tenseness in his attitude.

"Good God, look at that, something's wedged under there, something . . ." He looked uneasily towards Mrs. Abbott, and continued hastily, "No, I don't think I should come and look, Mrs. Abbott, it's some animal . . . something . . ."

Mrs. Abbott immediately made her way and looked down into the bubbling channel. "Blood?" she said. "That looks like blood, doesn't it? Disgusting. The wheel's stopped, something's wedged there, a rabbit, a dog, or a sheep. You didn't tell us this kind of thing happened when . . ."

"Nothing like this has ever happened before, to my knowledge," said the estate agent. "The wheel has always been turning, quickly if they're working, and slower, of course, if they're not, but it must be something bigger than a dog."

"A sheep, perhaps." Mrs. Abbott's voice was trembling slightly. "Or . . . a person . . . No one's ever fal— For God's sake." She walked along a little further and watched the wide stream of blood trickling along the channel, swirling about as it reached the eddies further along. She looked at Mr. Jensen, her eyes suddenly round and horrified. Mr. Jensen looked back at her, the same thought obviously coming into their heads at the same moment.

"Oh no, it's not, it can't be . . ." She turned round, gazed at the gate again, and called at the top of her voice, "Charles, Charles, where are you?" But there was no answer. She turned again and looked down at the water-mill, and at the same space between the mill and the mill-house, and then again at the blood, and she let out a long, long, piercing scream.

12

Sunday passed very peacefully for Carmichael. Again, she got up late as she had on Saturday, went through the same routine of morning tea and breakfast, but no cleaning. Sunday was decidedly a day of rest—a Church day . . . She felt brimful again of confidence, she was relaxed, no hay fever, she had slept well, it was wonderful. It was wonderful, this feeling.

She went to church; there was a new vicar and she wanted to see what kind of sermon he would preach. It was quite good really. She came to the conclusion, sitting there slightly apart from everyone else in her best summer frock, that he was a bit of a pacifist, and she wasn't one for that. She looked round the congregation smugly. "Thou shalt not kill" was quite right; she was absolutely against wars. After all, it was really just people making money out of armaments. But with her, of course, it was rather different.

Carmichael thought, with a sudden pang, of the Mini. She had driven straight back from Millstream House to her garage. She had to take it in next day, Monday, to get it repaired. She hadn't said anything about the man who had done it; she'd just said it was a hit and run, she didn't know who had done it. She'd gone back to her car and found it like that. After all, she could hardly say anything else, but he'd paid for it in one way, if he wasn't going to pay for it in another. The garage had said the glass wouldn't cost her much to have put back, and so far as she could see, there was no other scratch on the car. She brought her mind back and looked at the number of the hymn they were about to sing. The sermon had stopped and everybody stood up. Carmichael rose with them and started to sing the final hymn of the service.

As the organ pealed out the voluntary and the congregation were making their way out of church, Carmichael spoke to no one. She had only been to the church three times in her three months, and she looked round, slightly superciliously, and thought there was no one she wished to know any better. She took the clergyman's proffered hand at the door, made some murmured remark to his greeting, and then passed him by.

On the way down the path towards the pretty lych gate, she wondered if it would be a good plan to get the car out after lunch and run along the lane past Millstream House, just to have a look, just to see . . . But then she decided against it. After all, she didn't like the thought of taking the Mini out with a bashed headlamp. No, she wouldn't do that. She'd have a restful Sunday afternoon, and just wait to see what Monday brought forth.

Carmichael was looking forward to seeing the children's ward Sister again; she liked her, she was nice, Sister Jones, friendly. Yes, it might even be worth getting that bottle of sherry and asking her to the flat for a drink. She was longing to show the flat off to somebody, and Jones, well, she'd probably like to come. Yes, she quickened her pace towards home, that was a good idea; some time next week she'd get a bottle of sherry . . . It was so good to feel her old self again.

13

Monday morning was drizzling with rain. Carmichael got into the Mini, drove it out of the garage, trying not to think about the missing headlamp glass. She had an appointment this morning with her garage; it would be easy to get the bus the rest of the way to work. She drove along the road, avoiding people's eyes. One or two people she was sure glanced at her car, noting the number and finishing letter; a new car, and a broken headlight. What were their thoughts? They might put it down to her bad driving. She didn't want to meet their eyes.

She drove into the garage, and a young boy came forward; he recognized her. "O.K., miss. You're going to leave her then?"

Carmichael nodded. "I'll get the bus to the hospital. Will it be done by tonight?"

He shook his head. "Shouldn't think so. We've got your telephone number though, we'll ring you."

"I'm at the hospital, I'm a Sister." It still gave Carmichael pleasure to say that. He nodded but didn't appear impressed. "O.K. I'll ring there then. Got an extension number?"

"My office number is 86 Out Patients," said Carmichael primly, and he nodded again. She looked at his hands and didn't like to think of them, dirty and oily as they were, touching her car.

"Be careful with the upholstery on my car with those hands." Carmichael's voice was slightly louder, and the boy looked up sharply. "O.K., miss," he said, watching her as she walked out of the garage and along the road to the bus-stop. She glanced at her watch as she did so—twenty past eight; she'd be early. She'd have to go back by bus tonight, and probably to work the next morning, but anyway, all that had happened to her little car was very satisfactorily paid for. He won't bash any more cars, she thought compla-cently as she sat down with a bump in the corner seat of the bus, which started up rapidly as she got in. Thank goodness she didn't have to use these buses any more; they were uncomfortable after her car. She held her head high as she paid her money to the conductor; in spite of leaving the car behind her in the garage, in spite of the unimpressed young man, in spite of his oily hands, in spite of everything, she felt good.

14

Carmichael arrived at her department early and decided to go in by the front door rather than walk round through the hospital. That way, she'd get a glimpse of her nurses at work earlier than usual; she might surprise them at something. Shades of a past colleague doing this went through her mind. She grimaced a little.

She was right. Instead of the bustle that should have been taking place, the busy preparing for clinics, four nurses were clustered round the tea bar, leaning on it, talking. Carmichael stood in the doorway, their backs were to her; one was saying: "And I said to Jimmy, I was having none of that, I didn't believe in shacking up with people, I mean, why should you? After all, he's out of work, I'd be paying for . . ." Suddenly she sensed tension in the nurse who had glanced round at the door. They all turned round.

"Nothing to do, nurses? No clinics this morning? Everything been cancelled?" Carmichael's voice was sarcastic.

"No, Sister, we were just . . ."

"Just gossiping. Well don't. When you come on duty the idea is to prepare clinics, not to talk to each other about what happened the night before." The nurses dispersed.

Carmichael was walking through the department to go up to the hospital to the changing room and get into uniform when she passed Alice, the cleaner. Usually she'd disappeared by this time. She was slopping a cloth along the window-ledges of the waiting-room.

Carmichael walked up to her. "Alice, what are you supposed to be doing, cleaning with that dirty rag?" Alice whirled round. She looked about sixty-five or seventy, but was probably younger; the domestics weren't allowed to stay after sixty. Her grimy green overall, wet down the front; her sandals on stockingless feet showed none too clean toes peeping through the ends. The sandals themselves were greasy plastic.

Carmichael was disgusted. "If you can't do better than this, Alice, I shall have to ask for another cleaner."

Alice's eyes flashed with malice. "You can't do anything about it, we don't come under the Sisters now, not the domestics, we come under the supervisor, and a good job, I say." Alice wrung out the wet cloth in a noisome-looking bucket of water, picked it up and walked out of the department, slopping the water on the floor as she did so.

"H'm, then I'll speak to the supervisor," Carmichael said.

In the hospital, after she'd changed into her uniform, she walked back down the stairs, past the domestic supervisor's office. As she was passing, she decided it was a good idea to report Alice now. She knocked on the door.

Inside, Miss Hudson was sitting at her desk in a white coat. On her lapel was the insignia, Hudson, Domestic Supervisor. She looked up as Carmichael entered. "Yes, Sister. Something I can do for you?"

"Yes, you can remove the cleaner from Out Patients and give me somebody who cleans properly. I've just seen her slopping around with a filthy cloth and I won't have it."

The domestic supervisor ran her hand through her short, stubby black hair and glanced at the shelves of Harpic and cleaning materials round her, as if in search of another cleaner. "There isn't anyone else to give you. I've got three off sick, and we are short, you know they always disappear; they get a better job. It's as much as I can do to keep the wards' staff, let alone the departments'."

"And the departments come second, I suppose?"

"Well, no, not the operating theatre, but Out Patients isn't quite so important."

"Oh, isn't it? Well, it is to me." Carmichael, for the first time in her new hospital, felt she really had a chance to use her authority to some effect.

"Well, if you don't want Alice, I'll see who I can send you. I'll take Alice away if that's the way you feel about her. She's getting on, you know." The supervisor's voice was slightly reproving.

"If she's too old to work, she shouldn't be working," said Carmichael. "Don't send her back to me, I'll expect someone else tomorrow morning."

"It's difficult in a week to . . ." The domestic supervisor tailed off and a mulish expression came over her face as Carmichael walked out of the door, shutting it rather noisily behind her.

"Right," she said to the closed door. "I'll take Alice away, mate, but you will soon find out how long it is before you get another, and how will you like that?" She picked up the telephone.

Carmichael walked back to her own department, where the nurses were rushing about like beavers. She smiled; a word from her and things started humming. She went round each clinic critically. In the ear, nose, and throat clinic she ran her fingers along the glass of the trolley on which were arranged the instruments for examining and called to a nurse. "Nurse Pratt, what's the matter with this glass? It's not properly clean. Look, you can make a greasy mark on it with your finger. What have you cleaned it with?"

"Spirit, Sister," said the nurse, looking down at where Carmichael's finger had traced a line. "It does do that, it sort of makes a mark."

"It sort of makes a mark because it is not polished

enough, nurse. Elbow-grease, that's what you need, as well as the spirit, you know. Take all the instruments off and do it again."

"But Mr. Simm will be here in a minute, you know what he's like if things aren't ready, Sister."

"I do, so you'd better do it quickly, nurse." Carmichael walked on, oblivious to the face the nurse was pulling behind her back, but she heard the clatter of the instruments as the nurse cleared the trolley, preparatory to repolishing it.

There were not as many clinics on Monday morning, just the psychiatric clinic, and the two ear, nose, and throat clinics, one run by an ageing consultant, Mr. Simm, and the other by a clinical assistant, a good-looking young man the nurses ogled rather. That was another thing Carmichael must stop. She decided to put her oldest, least attractive nurse into that clinic. She called, "Nurse Baker."

"Yes, Sister." The elderly nurse, with grey hair and her cap slightly askew, put her head round the office door.

"I want you to take Dr. Easton's clinic this morning. I've decided to let Nurse Winter take the psychiatrist's."

"But I always take the psychiatrist's, Sister, and I don't know much about ear, nose, and throat, I don't know . . ."

Carmichael's steely look through her glasses silenced Nurse Baker. "Then all the more reason why you should learn, Staff," Carmichael said, dropping her eyes and looking at the list in front of her. "Go and tell Nurse Winter what I've said."

"She won't like it, Sister." Nurse Baker made a last effort; she knew Winter was keen on Dr. Easton, indeed she knew that he'd taken her out several times. It was a shame; she enjoyed that clinic, Winter did.

"Won't like it? Nurse Baker, we're not here to like or dislike, we're here to work." Carmichael's voice was dismissive, so Baker went.

In the E.N.T. clinic, next door to the one Carmichael had entered and found fault with the trolley, a pretty young nurse was putting the finishing touches to the clinic, hanging up a white coat behind the door, prising open the starched white pockets that were so stuck down when they came from the laundry that the doctors couldn't get anything in them unless they were first prised open. "Hallo, Baker, you look red in the face. What's the matter?" she asked.

"It's Sister, she says I'm to take Dr. Easton's clinic and you're to take the psychiatrist's."

For a minute there was a silence, then Winter broke out: "The old cow. She knows I like him. Mike'll be furious too, he likes me to take his clinic. We, well, we always make our date during the coffee-break. She can't do this to me, I'm going to say something, I really am."

"I shouldn't, I've already said something, or tried to, but she's adamant, and you know what she's like," said Baker defensively.

"I bloody do know what she's like, and I know why she's like it, because she can't get a man herself, that's why it is, she can't get a bloody man to look at her. And who would, anyway, with that face and the way she does her hair. She looks like . . . Oh, God, it makes you sick. I look forward to Monday mornings because of Mike, and that psychiatrist gets on my nerves, keeps you standing outside the door if there's anything juicy to listen to. All right, Baker, there you are," she said. "I suppose if you've got to take it, you've got to take it."

"I don't want to, I don't know anything about ear, nose, and throat; any snags?"

"Not with Mike, he's marvellous, he never gets shirty."

"Not with you, but what about me?" said Baker, and Winter looked up at her and grinned.

"Well, for God's sake, see there's no wax on the instruments when he's finished probing about, take them over to the sink and really scrub 'em. Even I've fallen down on that once or twice. You've got to be careful. And can you syringe ears?"

"Haven't for years," said Baker, a really frightened look on her face.

"Well, if I get the chance, I'll tell Mike, and maybe he'll do them himself. Don't worry. But I still can't get over it, that old bitch. If she could get a man of her own, she'd probably be nicer to everybody."

Winter flounced out of the clinic and made her way towards the clinic room at the further end of the department where the psychiatrist sat in state from ten to twelve-thirty. As she passed Carmichael's office, she gave her a malevolent look which Carmichael met from behind the glass of her office with an impassive face. Winter half-paused, was going to say something, then thought better of it. What was the use? This woman, you couldn't even talk to her. Holly, the last one, you could tell her your troubles, but this one— God, she was a bitch.

She flounced along, and Carmichael noticed the flounce and smiled to herself. Keep them in order, that's the thing, she thought. If they're frightened of you, they won't step out of line.

At lunchtime Carmichael watched Jones approaching her table with a loaded tray with some apprehension. She was wondering whether Jones had any news of Marie's father; perhaps she wouldn't, but Carmichael hoped. Jones put down her tray; on it was a plate of cold beef, potatoes, and rather grey-looking peas.

"Ugh, I hate Monday lunches," she said, "but have I got news for you!"

"News?" Carmichael looked up, a fork of mashed potatoes suspended between the plate and her mouth. "News? What news?" Her voice sounded innocent, but her heart was beating faster. She hoped to God that what she was going to hear was what she wanted to hear—that he was dead and hadn't just been injured and rushed into hospital.

"It's that bloody Abbott, he's dead. He's in the morgue. Well, they're cutting him up this afternoon, had to . . . B.I.D."

"When?" said Carmichael, trying to get exactly the right amount of surprise and curiosity in her voice.

"Brought in Sunday morning, got squashed in some mill or other. Charming, like raspberry jam, they said, had to scrape him off the wall." She shuddered. "I wouldn't wish that death on a dog. Wonder if he felt it?"

"No, he didn't." Carmichael started as she made her remark; she hadn't meant to.

"How do you know, for goodness' sake?" said Jones, looking at her curiously.

"That man wouldn't feel anything," said Carmichael.

Jones laughed. "Well, you may be right there," she said. "Anybody who could hit a kid like he did, well, he'd got no feeling, obviously, had he? But still . . . Fate, wasn't it? He'd gone to look at a new house, or something, and got squashed in this mill. I bet Mrs. Abbott's in a fair do, but anyway little Marie's safe. That's something, isn't it?"

Carmichael nodded and continued with her lunch silently. So he was dead. Well, that was just as it should be. She'd hoped that he wasn't just injured, but after all that blood she hadn't thought so. She wondered how the slim, elegant, rather vixenish Mrs. Abbott would take it. Perhaps she would be glad to be rid of him; you never knew in these cases. After all, if he bashed the kid, maybe they . . . Perhaps she enjoyed it though, seeing him do it, maybe they got their kicks that way. After all, people did get kicks from hurting other people, Carmichael knew that only too well. Well, she'd seen to it, she'd coped with it and that was that.

"Someone pranged my car at the weekend," she said. "Just broke the headlight. Probably it'll be ready tonight or tomorrow morning."

"Oh, hard," said Jones, as usual through a mouthful of food. "Hard luck. Injure the bodywork?"

Carmichael shook her head. "Just the glass," she said. "It won't be noticeable when they've fixed it, that's what the garage said."

"Good," said Jones. "They've got to do a P.M. on what's left of the body this afternoon; Abbott's, I mean," and she looked at Carmichael's preoccupied face.

"A P.M.? Oh yes, of course they'd have to, wouldn't they," said Carmichael, and she seemed to have lost all interest.

"By the way, Sister Jones, have you ever had a girl called Winter working for you in the children's ward?"

"Winter? Oh yes, quite a nice girl, rather pretty, used to flirt with the last House Physician."

"She flirts with anyone; I'm not too sure what kind of a report she'll get from me," said Carmichael.

"Oh. She seemed a good little nurse, the kids liked her, she did everything well, everything she was told to do she did properly," said Jones. "Don't you find her . . ."

Carmichael forestalled her. "Nevertheless . . ." she murmured.

Back in the department after lunch, Carmichael was met by Nurse Baker. "Your garage rang, Sister, and said your car would be ready if you liked to fetch it on your way home, about five-thirty. I said all right, I was sure you would. I hope I did right." Nurse Baker was still beaming after the morning clinic. She'd done well with Dr. Easton, he'd been charming to her, and no ear syringeing, thank God. She felt warm towards Sister Carmichael for moving her from the psychiatrist, which was probably the most boring clinic of the week.

Carmichael nodded; she felt pleased by the way Baker had said "Your garage phoned up, Sister."

"You did quite right, Staff Nurse Baker. Thank you, I'll call for it on the way home. How did you get on in the clinic this morning?"

"Very well, thank you, Sister. I liked it, it was a change from the psychiatrist, and as you said, one's got to be used to everything. It's just that I was a little nervous, you know, I was out of hospital so long until my husband died. It's very kind of you to try me in there."

Carmichael nodded. "Well, you can keep the clinic for the moment, but I won't say you can stay in it."

Nurse Baker nodded. "Thank you, Sister," she said.

"It would be a good idea, though, if you managed to wear your hat a little straighter," said Carmichael, and Baker hastily put her hand up to her cap.

"Yes, Sister, I'll go and have a look in the mirror and put it right." She dashed away. Carmichael smiled rather grimly. Someone liked her, anyway.

There was a crash from the clinic room, and Carmichael looked up sharply.

"Save the pieces, Mother liked the pattern." It was Baker's voice, strident with new confidence.

Carmichael grimaced, got up and went into the clinic room. "What's broken and who broke it?" she asked, looking round. Winter was there, Baker and Sutton, a very young cadet nurse. It was she who had dropped a specimen glass.

"Sorry, Sister, it slipped out of my hand. I was washing at the sink here, I turned round, and—"

"Very well, nurse, but see that all the pieces are picked up." Carmichael's voice was not so spiky as usual. The message from the garage, and Baker's attitude towards her, had for the moment introduced a little complacency into Carmichael. She turned away without further reproof.

The cadet walked out of the clinic room, along to the broom cupboard, and as she did so, Carmichael was reminded of something. She went back to her office, pulled the telephone towards her, took off the receiver and dialled a number. "Miss Hudson?" she said. The voice at the other end was obviously brief in its answer, for Carmichael went straight on. "I've had no cleaner at all today, I suppose you realize, Miss Hudson. It is imperative that the clinic rooms are clean; I expect the floors to be washed every day, you know that. And what about the operating theatre, that's not been touched. I can't let the nurses do it, you know that. How soon am I getting a cleaner here?"

The voice at the other end muttered something and Carmichael's nose twitched, and at the same time it began to run. She fumbled for a Kleenex. "I know I said I wouldn't have Alice, but that doesn't mean to say I won't have anyone. It's just as important that my theatre is kept clean; we're doing minor ops tomorrow afternoon. You know that it's got to be clean. You, after all, are the domestic supervisor, it's your job to see that each department and each ward has its cleaner. I'm sorry if I don't like the one you sent me. Where is she working now? Washing up on the wards in the evening. Well . . ." Carmichael's voice was slightly muffled, and she repeated, "I said, washing up on the wards in the evening. Well . . ." she said more clearly, and the phone, to her annoyance, was put down at the other end.

Carmichael was not at a loss. She would ring Major Johnson at the administrative centre. She dialled again, and a feminine voice answered.

"May I speak to Major Johnson, please?" said Carmichael. "Yes, it is urgent, very urgent." She waited, drumming her fingers on the desk impatiently. Afternoon clinics would soon be starting and she hadn't yet done her after-lunch round to see if they were properly laid up. She drummed a little more, then a man's voice came on the other end of the phone. "Yes, Sister?"

"I have no cleaner in the Out Patients department. It's a minor operation day tomorrow, I want the operating theatre properly cleaned. I've just rung Miss Hudson to ask for a cleaner, and she put the phone down. She may be short, but I'm afraid I cannot let my department go just because the domestic supervisor can't mobilize enough staff. I thought I had better get in touch with you, Major Johnson."

The administrative supervisor was obviously aware that there had to be a cleaner in Out Patients, but was just as sympathetic with Miss Hudson, that you can't make bricks without straw, and he ended up a rather lengthy conversation with Carmichael by saying that he would do his best. She put the phone down abruptly and got up and did her round of the clinics.

The afternoon clinics had all finished by five o'clock and the nurses cleared up and gone by half past. Carmichael looked round the department, went into each examination room and doctors' interview room, and closed and locked the windows. There was no need for her to do this; there was a porter laid on specially to come over at about six o'clock to see that nobody was left in the department and that it was locked, including the front door. Carmichael disliked this practice: she felt that the department was her own and therefore her responsibility. She went through the waiting-room, through the lobby to the outer doors, and pushed up the bolts, top and bottom, then came through and locked the inner doors. The sliding-glass window of the records office slid back, and a voice said: "Sister, I've locked this door and the one through into records, and Nurse Winter has gone over to get some shopping at the corner shop, and she was going to come through. You see, she won't be able to get through here, and if you've locked the outer door, she won't be able to get through there either. Do you mind unlocking your door, so that she can get in?"

Carmichael looked at her. "Yes, I do mind unlocking the doors. Nurse Winter should not go over to the shop in uniform; therefore, when she comes back, she'll find herself unable to get in. She will have to walk down the street, round to the front of the hospital, and come in at the front door. I'm sorry about it, but if she breaks the rules, that's her affair."

The records girl shrugged her shoulders, slipped on her coat, went out of her back door, and Carmichael heard it slam behind her. She smiled to herself; this could be worth waiting for.

She seated herself in one of the plastic chairs and flicked through a magazine. It was rather interesting to get a patient's-eye view of the place; it all looked rather nice. The clock said twenty to six and suddenly there was a rattle on the front door. Carmichael turned round and looked. It was Winter, in uniform, with a heavy shopping bag in her hand. Well . . .

The nurse pressed her face against the glass door; she could see through into the department and Carmichael sitting in the chair with a magazine in her hand. She took a coin from her pocket and rapped noisily on the glass door. Carmichael didn't move. Nurse Winter walked away from that door, obviously to try the records office door, with similar results, then came back again. This time she knocked a little harder on the glass door, but Carmichael had gone.

In the Sisters' changing room Carmichael slipped her uniform clothes into her locker, put on her dress, and then went to the mirror to look at herself. The exchange with Winter, the triumph that she felt in catching someone out, had made a slight flush appear on her cheeks and did something to counteract the red-edged lids and the red-tipped nose. Her eyes, too, sparkled a little with the same triumph and her lips curled upwards. She did an unusual thing; she took out her lipstick from her bag and put a little more on than usual. Normally she didn't bother when she was going home, but perhaps she would bother. She really felt exhilarated by the encounter with Winter, and she was well aware, exhilarated by the fact that she had put another problem right. She thought of Winter; prettiness wasn't everything. She tossed her head and watched herself in the mirror. Unfortunately her bun began to uncoil, and this brought her mood down. She pulled out a few hairpins, recoiled the meagre bun at the back of her neck, and stuck the pins fiercely back in.

16

Major Abbott's death caused little stir in Dwyford. A description of his rather gruesome end did make the national press, but only with a very small paragraph. The local paper, of course, was a little more concerned, and a three-quarter-length column under the headline "Man Crushed to Death Under Water-wheel" described his macabre end, listed his army record, and the fact that he left a wife and a three-year-old child. That, and the small account of the time he had been in Dwyford as an accountant and that the cremation would take place at three o'clock, etc., etc., completed the piece.

Some people in Dwyford were more stirred and irritated by the fact that the house where they purchased their granary bread and flour was closed, perhaps out of respect for the dead, or more likely due to the fact that they'd had partially to dismember the wheel to get the body out. This, of course, was not in the paper, but the owner of the mill told would-be customers the details with some relish, knowing full well that it would have little effect on his trade, as, of course, the crushing had happened outside the mill, not inside.

Within a week the whole thing was over and forgotten, and two old ladies who were found in a gas-filled room, one with her head bashed in, decidedly pushed all thought of Major Abbott into the background.

In St. Matthew's, too, the incident was soon forgotten. Only a few nurses and Dr. Stephenson and the House Physician had really come into much contact with Major Abbott, and their feelings were mostly of relief, like Sister Jones'. After all, the problem appeared, as it were, to have solved itself, and little Marie Abbott was safe, without any more of the annoying, time-consuming inquiries having to be pursued.

Much the same feeling was felt by the social workers engaged on Marie's case. The few times one of them had called at the Abbotts' house and made inquiries among their neighbours, they had been made anything but welcome and had also made little progress. The suburban area in which the Abbotts lived did not welcome this kind of thing, and so the social workers were pleased, too, that little Marie was safe and the case could be dropped.

17

Carmichael was getting more and more furious about the fact that Miss Hudson had not so far found her a cleaner. Out Patients was getting decidedly dirty. In the middle of the week, having rung Miss Hudson every morning and received the same evasive reply, she decided to go up to the office. "I won't be long, I'm just going to see Miss Hudson," she said to Nurse Baker, who was tidying the magazines on the table preparatory to going to lunch.

She answered: "Yes, Sister, all right, Sister." Carmichael despised Baker, yet found the constant use of her title gratifying . . . At the back of her mind she saw herself, Carmichael, talking to Marion Hughes, the Night Superintendent at her last hospital, and so, although it was gratifying, she still despised Baker's attitude.

She marched out of the department, through the hospital, up the stairs, and banged heavily on Miss Hudson's door.

"Come in," said a weary, somewhat exasperated voice. Carmichael opened the door, walked in, and stood in front of Miss Hudson.

"Miss Hudson, it is imperative that I have a cleaner tomorrow morning. The place is filthy, and I shall have to report it elsewhere."

"You've already done that. You rang up the head supervisor, didn't you? I know, he came down on me, but he understands the situation far better than you do, Sister Carmichael. At the moment I have no one but Alice; if you would like to have Alice back, I will be delighted to send her tomorrow."

"Why, won't anyone else have her?"

"Please sit down, Sister." Hudson looked up, putting her hand, as she always did, through her black hair and scratching violently the top part of her head. Carmichael shook her head and refused to take the offered seat.

"Look, Sister Carmichael, I know it's difficult for you, I know that Alice isn't the best of cleaners, but we are at the moment in quite a state. We have three off sick."

"You said that before," Carmichael broke in. "Are there always three off sick, or is it the same three off sick? If so, why don't you get someone else to replace them, if that's the case?"

"No, it isn't the case. It's three more who are off sick, and the other three have returned, but that makes no difference to my numbers, does it? Also, you know very well the establishment has been cut, and we have to put up with what we've got. Alice is all I've got. If you won't take her back, I can't help you at the moment. I'm sorry. I know it's difficult. I will send someone down this evening to clean the theatre, after six."

"That's no good. I won't be there, and I don't like people in the department after I've left, and I can't supervise her cleaning."

"It is not your job, Sister, to supervise the cleaning, it is mine," said Miss Hudson, obviously trying to keep her patience. "And as to having someone in the department when you're not there, the last Out Patients Sister . . ."

"I am not the last Out Patients Sister, I am the present Out Patients Sister, and I do not want anyone in the department after I have left it. That is absolutely that," said Carmichael, and her voice rasped.

Miss Hudson looked up at her, shook her head, and rested her chin on her hands. "You know, Sister Carmi-

chael, if I may say so," she said, "I know this is your first
Sister's post, but it would be far easier if you were less
adamant."

"It may be my first Sister's post, but I think it is very, very
wrong of you to bring such a thing up. I shall report it to the
S.N.O.," said Carmichael icily. "But if I don't get a cleaner
within the next few days, I shall tell the doctors that they
can't do minor ops in the theatre because it is too dirty to
use." This was a weapon that Hudson had to recognize as
being valid.

"I will send the cleaner tonight at six o'clock, as I have
said. She's a good cleaner and will do the job properly.
Also, I will stay on to see that she does it properly, all
right?"

"I suppose it's got to be all right," said Carmichael. "But
I shall complain to the head supervisor again if I am not
given a cleaner, and if that fails I shall go to the planning
officer."

"The planning officer has nothing to do with it," Miss
Hudson broke in.

"I said I will go to the planning officer and I will. He,
perhaps, can do something with the head domestic supervisor." Carmichael's mouth was a straight, thin line, and
Hudson looked at her with dislike.

"You must do as you wish, Sister, but your theatre will be
cleaned tonight and that is as far as I can go unless you are
willing to take Alice back."

"Which I am not," said Carmichael, "and that's final,
Miss Hudson. She makes the department dirtier after she
has been through it than it was before, with that filthy rag. I
am surprised that you . . ."

"I don't want to be told my duties, Sister Carmichael; if
you don't mind, I've got work to do." Miss Hudson started
to shuffle the papers on her desk and got up and looked at a
rota board hanging beside the shelves of Harpic.

"Very well, we shall see." Carmichael opened the door and walked out, slamming it behind her, but not before she had heard Miss Hudson sigh, and mutter, "Now, who the hell can I take away from a ward tonight to clean that bloody Out Patients theatre?"

Carmichael walked away from the closed door. "It had better be someone," she said under her breath, and then she remembered something. Miss Hudson had a white Triumph car just like Marion Hughes. Pity, though, she didn't come to the canteen for her coffee. Carmichael gave a little laugh . . . then shook her head as her thoughts went on. No, that wouldn't do. Two alike, never, that would be very suspicious. She smiled, quite broadly for Carmichael . . . Miss Hudson was the kind of person who . . . well, the place, the world would be better without . . . incompetent and stubborn.

18

The week progressed with no regular cleaner, although Carmichael found that the theatre was being cleaned after she had left in the evening. A critical inspection of the walls and floor, the operating table and glass shelves, revealed no hidden dirt, so Carmichael had to be satisfied, but the rest of the department was anything but clean.

On the Tuesday morning of the following week, Carmichael went into the nurses' clinic room, where the urine-testing, weighing and measuring of patients, giving of injections, and the few dressings that were needed in an Out Patients department were done. She looked round critically. Staff Nurse Baker was swabbing down the tops of the working surfaces.

"You're not supposed to do that, Staff Nurse," said Carmichael, but her voice was mild, for she knew only too well that there was no one else to do it.

"I know, Sister," replied Baker unctuously. "But if it gets absolutely filthy, somebody has got to do it. I know if our Nursing Officer saw me, she'd have something to say, I suppose, but I feel like this: it's due to you to have the place clean, and I shall just, if you don't mind, do it when no one's looking. Is it all right?" She smiled her rather stupid smile at Carmichael, who nodded and looked round the rest of the room.

She ran her finger along the top of the locked drugs cupboard and looked at her finger. It was encrusted with dust. "Something will have to be done, Staff Nurse," she said. "I can't go on like this. No, I didn't mean you," as Baker came over with her damp cloth, reached over, and rubbed it across the top of the cupboard.

"It's really too much, I'm absolutely disgusted." She looked round the floor, which was also none too clean. Then she spied something shining, wedged between the clinic-room cupboard and the wall. She bent down and tried to dislodge it with her fingers. Something tinkled to the floor; it was quite a large concave piece of glass, about an inch and a half across. Carmichael jumped back hastily, nearly knocking Baker over, with a cry of pain, and Baker saw the blood oozing from Carmichael's finger.

"Oh, Sister, you've cut your finger, wait a minute."

Carmichael went over to the sink and turned the cold tap on the oozing wound. "Don't make a fuss, Nurse Baker, it's nothing," she said. "Give me a Band-Aid."

But as the water flowed, she saw that a little more than a Band-Aid would be necessary, and Baker, inspecting it, saw it, too. She went over to another cupboard, opened it, and took out a small dressing pack, tore the top off, and put a large piece of gauze over the wet finger.

"You'll have to have a stitch in that, Sister, it looks quite deep to me."

"Wait a minute, let me get a good look," said Carmichael, and she removed the gauze, while Baker stood poised to put another piece of gauze over the cut when Carmichael had finished inspecting it. The cut was about an inch long and quite deep.

"If this place had been cleaned properly, that wouldn't have happened. It must have been lying there for ages."

"It was a piece of that specimen glass, I expect. Do you remember, the one the cadet nurse broke last week; that's what it is, Sister."

"I hope it was washed properly, then. It can't be very clean, anyway, if it's been lying there for a week or more."

Baker shook her head sympathetically. "Better go over to Casualty, Sister, and let them have a look at it, I would," she said.

Carmichael cradled the injured hand against her other arm. "I think I will, it does look a bit deep, and it might have been dirty. Perhaps I'd better have a shot of penicillin as well. Anyway, I'll see what the Casualty Officer says. Look after things, Nurse Baker, while I'm gone."

"Of course, Sister." Nurse Baker was obviously pleased. She wasn't even senior nurse, but Sister seemed to favour her; not many Sisters had before.

Carmichael walked through the department, down a long corridor, into the hospital, along past the pharmacy, and through the lobby, into Casualty. There were several people in the waiting-room, but she stalked through and rang the bell. The door opened immediately.

"Yes?" a nurse said, hardly looking at her, then, realizing it was Sister Carmichael of Out Patients, she went on hastily, "Oh yes, Sister, have you done something to yourself?"

"I'd hardly be here with a piece of gauze round my finger if I hadn't, nurse," Carmichael said coldly, and the nurse hastily opened the door further.

"Please come through, Sister," she said, and Carmichael went through.

The Casualty Sister looked up from a form she was filling in at her desk. "Hallo, Carmichael, what have you been doing to yourself? Sit down."

Carmichael sat down in the chair beside the Casualty Sister's desk. "I've cut my finger on a piece of glass. I thought I'd better let the Casualty Officer see it, it looks as if it could do with a stitch."

"O.K. I'll get him, he's just looking at a kid in there, won't be a minute." She got up and walked through into the dressing area, and came back accompanied by the young Casualty Officer.

"Hallo, Sister, in the wars?" Carmichael silently held out her hand and he folded back the gauze. "M-m, how did you do that?" he asked.

"On a piece of glass. I don't even know if it was clean," said Carmichael.

"O.K. It needs a couple of sutures, I'll do them myself," he said to the Sister. "Better have some penicillin, too, I think, and some antitetanus, O.K.? Have you had antitetanus before?"

Carmichael got up and they went through, talking, into the Casualty operating theatre, where a nurse greeted Sister Carmichael. "Would you mind getting up on the table, it's easier," she said.

Carmichael obeyed, twitching her skirt down fussily as she did so. The nurse thrust a board in on the right side of the table under Carmichael's shoulder, and Carmichael automatically stretched her hand out on to it and lay there passively.

"Half a minute, I'll put the head-rest up a bit, no need for you to lie flat," said the nurse chattily. Sister Carmichael nodded.

The nurse wheeled the trolley up to the right-hand side of the theatre table, and Carmichael looked at it with some distaste and found herself feeling a twinge of fear.

The doctor, who had by this time reached her side, looked at her. "Don't worry, I'll give you a local. I know what you Sisters are, scared stiff of the needle, eh? You look the other way," he smiled and Carmichael turned her head away. After a few moments, she felt the fine anaesthetic needle being driven into the side of the cut.

"All right, Sister?" asked the Casualty Officer, and Carmichael nodded. She hardly felt the suturing needle go in, only a pressure on her finger. Then the Casualty Officer's cheerful voice said, "O.K. I've put two sutures in. You'll have to keep it dry, you know. Dressing, please, nurse."

The nurse dressed the finger with tuba-gauze and tied it neatly, but Carmichael looked at the finger in some annoyance. "Does it have to be as big as that—the dressing, I mean?" The nurse looked at the doctor questioningly.

"Well, it is a bit bulky," he said. "But leave it for a couple of days and then we'll probably put on something smaller. You'll get your stitches out in four or five days, don't worry."

"Very well, doctor," Carmichael said primly. She was thinking of driving the Mini with that finger up in the air, and walking round the department with it. It was humiliating, somehow, for a Sister to have a bandaged finger. She didn't like it, particularly as it was all due to Miss Hudson. She wondered if she should call at her office again on her way back to the department and tell her what had happened, but decided against it. She felt slightly queasy, which was stupid, of course. She thanked the Casualty Officer, who nodded absently and walked out of the theatre. After the penicillin and antitetanus injections she got off the table, pulled up her knickers, and pulled down her dress, settling it primly on her hips as well as she could with the dressing on her finger.

"She's certainly put you a nice big dolly on," said the Casualty Sister, smiling.

"Yes, it's going to be a great nuisance. I think she could have put on something smaller."

"Well, we won't hurt her feelings by taking it off today, but if you like to pop over the day after tomorrow, I'll put you on something smaller, all right?" The Casualty Sister looked at Carmichael inquiringly.

"Yes, I'll come over about ten o'clock. Thank you." Carmichael turned and whisked out of the theatre, through the waiting-room, and off to her own department, leaving the Casualty Sister still standing in the theatre. She threw the spirit swab into the dressing bucket and automatically broke the top of the disposable syringe, put the cap on it, and flung that after the swab.

"Queer fish, that," she said to herself, and the Casualty nurse, who had just walked into the theatre to clear up the suture trolley, looked at Sister curiously.

"Did you say something, Sister?" she asked, but the Casualty Sister just smiled, shook her head, and went back to her desk.

19

Next morning Carmichael came on duty feeling slightly depressed. It was not a morning she liked, and her finger had throbbed all night. She was greeted with a new cleaner, which lifted her spirits a little.

"Good morning," she said in her frosty manner, and the woman turned round, looked her up and down, and answered, "Morning. Name's Dixon, Mrs. Dixon."

Carmichael nodded, and watched the woman, with a slightly cleaner rag than Alice's, clean the window-ledges. "Has the theatre been done, and the nurses' clinic room?" she asked.

"Yes, it 'as. The theatre was done last night, and I dun the clinic room this morning, and a nice mess it was in," said the cleaner nastily, and she walked off through the waiting-room and was about to turn into Sister's office.

"Haven't you done my office? I like that done first, before I come on duty." Carmichael's voice was terse.

"Well, you may do, but I don't know the routine. All right, I'll leave it then, and do it tomorrow." The woman walked off down the corridor, singing softly to herself, and Carmichael shrugged. She looked at the thin film of dust over her desk and the top of her file, and thought it would be better to keep that till tomorrow than have the woman dusting and she having to wait outside. Not a good image to present to her nurses, who were bustling about getting the orthopaedic clinic ready.

"We've no draw sheets, Sister, and no dressing towels. I

don't know what's happened to the laundry, nothing's come this morning." Nurse Wanstead, the Jamaican nurse, thrust her head round Sister's office doorway.

"I'll ring up," said Carmichael, and pulled the phone towards her. "No laundry has been delivered yet. What's happened?" This should have been trundled round by a porter from the central laundry supply early in the morning. It was usually dumped in the last cubicle, but this morning apparently—nothing.

"Been a bit of a problem, porter's off sick, it'll be round soon."

"No dressing packs, either, Sister, or syringes. I ordered them yesterday." The Jamaican nurse, still standing there, looked at Sister with raised eyebrows and then smiled.

"What a nuisance. Well, I'll ring them, too," said Carmichael. "I don't know what is happening to everybody, the inefficiency is disgraceful."

"It's going to be one of those mornings, Sister. It always is when the orthopods come, isn't it? I don't know why, they seem to bring a jinx with them." Carmichael nodded; it was true, orthopaedic mornings always seemed to go wrong. For a start, usually the orthopaedic surgeons were late, took hours over their coffee, talking about their cases and going into long, passionate discussions as to whether a patient broke his hip and fell, or fell and broke his hip. Carmichael understood, of course, that these things must be gone into, and the clinical aspect looked at; but really she wished they wouldn't do it in the middle of seeing patients.

Carmichael had heard that Holly Newman used to go in and literally break it up, or have coffee with them so that she could wheedle them back to work, but Carmichael would have none of that. She had her coffee alone, in her office. She certainly didn't want to get familiar with the consultants, or so she told herself, but basically she knew she was slightly nervous of meeting them on even such a social level as coffee in the clinic.

At ten o'clock no one had appeared, and the nurses came back from their early morning coffee-break and were talking in the clinic room. Carmichael could do little about this, because there was nothing else for them to do until the surgeons arrived, and she clicked her tongue impatiently, then remembered her finger. She would go over and have the dressing changed now. She looked at the tuba-gauze. It was slightly dirty, even though she had taken the precaution of putting a cellophane dressing over it while she was in her flat.

"I'm just going over to Casualty to have this dressing redone," she called to a Staff Nurse passing her office.

The nurse paused. "Oh, Sister, I do hope it's all right, I hope it's not too sore." The nurse looked at Carmichael with a sincere and caring glance and Carmichael nodded briefly.

"I won't be long," she said.

In Casualty only a few "dressings" were sitting in the waiting-room, and Carmichael walked straight through, didn't ring the bell, just opened the door and walked in. Sister looked up. "Good morning, Sister." She obviously didn't remember the finger, then recalled it. "Oh, sorry, of course, you came over, didn't you, yesterday, to have your finger sutured. All right, is it?"

"No, it throbbed all night. It was very painful; I was going to have the dressing changed tomorrow, but it's so bulky I thought . . ."

"Oh, I'm sorry about that, I should have given you something to take, a Mogadon or something. A finger can be quite painful."

"I don't take sleeping pills," said Carmichael, and the Casualty Sister was, as it were, stopped in her tracks.

She looked straight at Carmichael and then said, "Well,

Sister, come into the dressing-room and I'll put on a smaller dressing anyway. That will probably make it more comfortable."

Carmichael followed her through into the dressing-room, sat down beside one of the couches, and Sister went off to fetch a dressing pack. She came back, pulled the curtains along so that the dressing of the finger would not be too public. The tuba-gauze came off easily in one piece and the sutures were revealed.

"Looks nice and clean," said Sister, expertly tearing the top off the dressing packet, extracting a piece of gauze with forceps and laying it over the finger. "Now, I think if we strap that on with two pieces of strapping, it will be less cumbersome, don't you?"

Carmichael nodded, and as the Sister was about to cut a piece of strapping from the roll she held in her hand, a nurse put her head round the curtain. "Ambulance, Sister, nasty case, little girl, fallen down or something."

The sister made a face at Carmichael. "Won't be a minute, better go and see," she said, and left Carmichael behind the half-drawn curtain. She sat there, interested. Casualty was an exciting place. She wondered how she'd like to be a Sister in a Casualty department, and was sure that she would be extremely efficient at the job.

"Right-ho, bring her through; no, leave Mother in the waiting-room for the moment." Carmichael heard Sister's brisk, pleasant voice, and then a trolley was wheeled into the dressing-room. Carmichael stood up, the better to see the occupant. It was a small girl. Her fair hair was tousled round her head and a large dressing covered the forehead and one eye, the other eye was closed and blackened, the mouth was swollen and the lower lip badly split. Carmichael noticed cuts, too, on the chin, and that the corner of a red blanket over the legs was folded back and a green towel over one leg, which meant injury there as well. Carmichael sat down again.

Awful, a road traffic accident, she supposed; knocked down. Well, she would be in the children's ward in no time, and she was glad it wasn't she who was looking after the children's ward that night. The child was obviously badly injured. It took her mind back to St. Jude's again, her old hospital. There she had had children in the ward, the results of road traffic accidents. Horrible. How she had hated it. Thank God that part of her nursing career was over. Never again would she take on a children's ward.

Carmichael watched the trolley being wheeled up to the couch and the curtains being drawn round. She could hear the ambulance men gently lifting the child on to the couch, then the trolley was pulled out and they disappeared from the department, taking the trolley with them. Both men, as they passed Carmichael, looked particularly grim.

"Get the kid's notes, will you." A doctor walked in hastily, followed by another, the orthopaedic House Officer. Carmichael recognized him; he should be over taking a clinic in her department now. Obviously they'd known this case was coming in.

"Get the notes, for God's sake," she heard the doctor's voice again, irritable.

"She's gone to get them, the clerk's gone to get them from the records office and she won't be a minute," a nurse's voice from behind the screen spoke to the doctor placatingly.

At that moment another nurse walked through and also went behind the screen. Carmichael heard her say, "I've got the particulars off the mother, I thought I'd better while the clerk was getting the notes. After all, it always takes time. She's been in before, mother said, in the ward. Her name is Marie Abbott."

Carmichael pricked up her ears. Marie Abbott, bashed

again, no. He was dead, he couldn't have done that. She stood up again to try and see better. It was obvious that the Casualty Sister had forgotten her, and at that moment another casualty was brought in. Carmichael was anxious to hear more about the child, so she didn't remind them of her presence.

"Here they are, here are the notes, sir." The department clerk, in her white coat, handed the notes through the curtain to the doctor. Carmichael heard him give a low whistle. "Don't like this. Where's the mother?" The doctor's voice was urgent.

"In the waiting-room," Carmichael heard the nurse answer.

"Look, take her up to the rest-room, the mother. I think I'd better call Stephenson, it may be . . ." He put his head round the curtains to see if anyone else was in the Casualty dressing-room, saw that another patient had been brought in, and said no more. Carmichael had heard enough. So-o-o, it hadn't been the father who was beating the child up, but the mother. Well, that was strange. The child's plight meant really very little to Carmichael, but she thought fleetingly what Jones' reaction would be . . . She'd go right up the wall.

She pulled back the curtain that was hiding her from the nurses passing to and fro. "Could I have my dressing finished, please, and get back to my department?" she asked.

"Oh, Lord. Sorry, didn't know you were there, Sister." The nurse came up to Carmichael and pushed the trolley that Sister had left nearer to her.

"Sister said just two pieces of strapping would be all right."

The nurse quickly and expertly cut off two pieces and finished the dressing neatly. Carmichael thanked her and walked out of the dressing-room, through the lobby by Sister's desk, and out into the waiting-room. There she saw the trim figure of Mrs. Abbott disappearing through the further door. Mrs. Abbott going up to the rest-room, thought Carmichael to herself. Then, looking sideways, she saw a smart leather handbag standing on the chair. Obviously Mrs. Abbott had left it behind. There was no other person in the waiting-room who looked like the owner of such an opulent article.

"That lady who nurse has just taken to the rest-room has left her handbag," said Carmichael to a nurse who was just handing a walking-stick to a patient, who had obviously been to have his ankle rebandaged.

"Oh, blast," said the nurse. "I guess I'll have to rush up to the rest-room with it."

At that moment the Casualty doors opened and another trolley was wheeled in.

"O.D.," said the ambulance man succinctly. "Got the bottle and what's left of the pills; shall I take her through?"

The door opened and Casualty Sister walked into the waiting-room, looking slightly harassed. "What's this?" she asked.

"An overdose, Sister; got the bottle. Shall I take her through to the theatre?"

"Oh, God in Heaven, why can't she go straight to the medical ward? We're pretty busy," said Sister.

"Tried. Medical ward won't have her, they say they've got two extra beds up now and they can't cope. Anyway, they won't do the stomach wash-out down there, it'll have to be here."

"Who by, for God's sake?" said Sister as two more casualties trooped in, one dripping blood copiously from a finger, and the other with a handkerchief clamped to a bleeding nose.

"Typical," said Casualty Sister. "Why the hell they can't do a wash-out down there in bed, I don't know. They must know what it's like here. All right, wheel her through to the theatre. Nurse, take the O.D. trolley in there and start that wash-out, I'll be with you." She turned to Carmichael and shrugged comically. "I don't know," she said. "Who'd be a Casualty Sister?"

"Mrs. Abbott has left her bag there, I'll have to take it to the rest-room, Sister." Sister looked at the nurse whom she had asked to go through with the O.D., but before she had time to reply, Carmichael cut in. "Don't worry, Sister, I'll take it up for you."

"Oh, that is decent of you," said the Casualty Sister. "The other one's not back from the rest-room yet. Ah, here she is."

At that moment the nurse who had accompanied Mrs. Abbott walked in. "She left her handbag behind her, I was going . . ."

"Never mind, you should have seen she'd got everything before you took her up," said the Casualty Sister, and went on, "Sister Carmichael's going to take it up for us. You get into the dressing-room and get on with some of those dressings. There's an R.T.A. in as well as a little girl," and she put her head back through the door and called the clerk. "Come and get these particulars down, for goodness' sake."

She disappeared as the clerk came out into the waiting-room and the nurse said hastily, "Thanks, Sister," to Carmichael as she passed her on her way to the dressing-room. Carmichael picked up the handbag and walked out of the department.

As she walked along the corridor and then proceeded up the stairs to the rest-room, she was surprised at the weight of the bag. She looked back to see if anyone was following her along the corridor which led to the wards before she turned right to a smaller passage leading to the rest-room. The rest-room was set aside for relatives who needed to be kept in the hospital because a patient was in some danger, or for patients who had to wait a long time. It was a small, comfortable room, with a bed, two or three armchairs, some reading matter, and if the patient's relative was suddenly bereaved, a nurse or someone who could provide tea and comfort.

Carmichael snapped open the expensive leather handbag. Inside, crushed against the leather lining, was a purse, a cheque-book, a wallet of some kind, and a driving licence. But what was making the bag so heavy was a half-bottle of whisky. Carmichael smiled to herself, snapped the bag shut, tapped on the rest-room door, and entered.

Mrs. Abbott was seated on the edge of one of the armchairs; she looked nervous and shaky.

"I've brought your handbag, Mrs. Abbott. You left it in Casualty."

Mrs. Abbott looked up at Carmichael. A strange expression came over her face that Carmichael could not define or explain. "Oh, thank you, thank you so much, I was wondering where it was. I was just going down to try and find it." Her voice shook as she took the handbag and put it on her knee, her hand restlessly running to and fro across the handle. She's waiting for me to go so that she can have a quick swig, thought Carmichael with contempt, so she stood there, watching.

"I'm sorry about your little girl, she seems to have had quite an . . . accident," Carmichael said.

Mrs. Abbott looked up again, suspiciously this time. "Yes, she tumbled down the stairs, it was such a bump. She rushes about, you know, she's a very over-active child, she stumbled and fell, from top to bottom of the stairs. It was dreadful."

Carmichael noticed that Mrs. Abbott's hands were trembling. "Yes, poor little Marie, she's been in before, hasn't she?" Carmichael's eyes were fixed steadily on Mrs. Abbott's face.

"Yes, she's what they call accident-prone; indeed, Dr. Stephenson thought she might have some disease of the bones, *fragilitas* something, I can't remember."

Carmichael nodded. "Yes . . . It must have been quite a fall, quite a tumble." Carmichael smiled her downward smile at Mrs. Abbott, walked to the door, opened it, and closed it softly behind her. She didn't leave the vicinity of the rest-room, but waited, listened. Mrs. Abbott, inside, snapped open the handbag. She gave her a few seconds more, then quietly twisted the handle of the door, opened it, and put her head round. Mrs. Abbott was just in the act of drinking from the mouth of the bottle. As Carmichael's face appeared, she hastily took the bottle away from her lips and put it down by the side of the chair, away from Carmichael, her face reddening perceptibly.

"I wondered if you'd like me to ask nurse to bring you up a cup of tea, but it seems . . ." Carmichael's voice was mildly sarcastic.

"No, no thank you, it's all right." Mrs. Abbott almost snapped, although her voice was still shaky.

Carmichael looked at her, a long, contemptuous look. Their eyes met like two antagonists'. Mrs. Abbott held the glance well, to Carmichael's surprise, but she was the first to drop her eyes. Carmichael withdrew, closed the door behind her, leant against it for a second or two with a satisfied smirk, and then made her way back to her own department.

When she arrived back, the clinics were in full swing. The orthopaedic surgeon and his registrar had arrived, late because they had both been to Casualty to look at Marie's leg; obviously, by the look of the waiting-room, things were not too far behind. Carmichael walked into one clinic after the other, looking at the appointments list, comparing it with the names of the patients waiting to be examined. No, things were not too far behind.

"Is your finger all right, Sister?" Staff Nurse Baker, of course. Carmichael nodded abruptly, and then turned to greet the Nursing Officer who was doing a round.

"Sister Carmichael," she said briskly. "I came before, but you were in Casualty having your finger dressed. I hear you cut it, the day before yesterday, was it? On duty?"

"Yes, Miss Excell, I cut it on a piece of glass. I put it in the accident book, of course."

"Good. I suppose they've given you all the treatment you should have in Casualty?" Miss Excell was a pleasant woman, and she looked at the dressing on Carmichael's finger. "Not too bad by the look of it. Stitches?"

Carmichael nodded. "Just two," she said. "It was slightly painful yesterday but it's better now. I was just going to have a cup of coffee. Will you join me?" The Nursing Officer nodded. Carmichael didn't know her well, and wished to know her better. It was always as well to be in with the seniors. Miss Excell went into Carmichael's office, sat down in the spare chair, and looked critically down at her navy dress, and with her hand brushed some lint from it.

When Carmichael came back with two cups of coffee, she asked, "Have you got a clothes-brush? I've been in the children's ward, and I must have got some gauze or something on my dress." She picked at one or two threads, and Carmichael, as if by magic, whisked a clothes-brush from one of the drawers and handed it to her.

"Thanks," said Miss Excell, brushed the front of her dress, and handed the brush back to Carmichael, who popped it back in the drawer and closed it again.

"Well equipped, eh?" smiled Miss Excell, then said "Thanks" as Carmichael handed her a cup of coffee.

"Sugar?" asked Carmichael, and Miss Excell nodded.

"Shouldn't, but do," she said, putting in two heaped teaspoonsful, raising her eyes comically to Carmichael as she did so.

"It doesn't seem to hurt your figure, Miss Excell," said Carmichael.

Miss Excell grimaced. "No, I don't seem to get fat, thank goodness, which is just as well, as I love sweet things, chocolates, sugar. How are you liking it here? We haven't really seen much of each other yet. How long have you been here now?"

"It's over three months," said Carmichael. "Yes, I'm liking it very much."

There was a pause, then Carmichael spoke again. "Did you know little Marie Abbott is in Casualty again?"

"Yes, it's dreadful, absolutely dreadful. Of course, nothing is definitely proved yet, but there seem to be some funny injuries from falling downstairs."

"Bad?" Carmichael was really not very interested, but after all, Miss Excell would be deeply concerned, and it was just as well to show interest in anything that was of importance to a senior.

"Compound fracture of one leg, almost unknown in a child, broken wrist, not too bad, a badly blackened eye, and the eyelid cut, and, most peculiar thing, cuts right across the eyelid, needs a plastic surgeon, I should think. The eye's not damaged though, thank God." Miss Excell sipped her coffee and continued, "I didn't get any coffee this morning. I usually have it in my office, but what with one thing and another I didn't get it. Casualty's busy."

"Yes, it was busy when I was over there. They'd just had an O.D. brought in as I came out," said Carmichael.

"Yes, the medical ward is full, too." Miss Excell finished her coffee and put the empty cup back on the tray on Carmichael's desk. "Thanks anyway, that's a relief, now I can get on," she said.

"What will happen about Marie; I mean Marie Abbott, what will be the next thing? I used to be on a children's ward, but, thank goodness, I never had anything like Marie brought in."

"Well, no one has proved it is 'anything like this,' as you put it, Sister," said Miss Excell, "but between you and me I think it's pretty certain. It's a case of baby-bashing all right. No child ever got injuries like that falling down the stairs, and this is the third time, too."

"What will happen then? I mean, what's the procedure now?" Carmichael asked again.

"Oh, the usual. There'll be a primary case conference with all the people involved, like the social workers and the health visitor, probably her G.P. I don't know. They'll rope in anyone who has ever had anything to do with the family. Of course, it's unfortunate that Mrs. Abbott's just lost her husband, one feels a bit sorry for her with regard to that."

"Then what?" asked Carmichael.

"Oh, a couple more visits from the health visitor and social workers, then another case conference, then I suppose they'll have to see her G.P. and get him to recommend her to see a psychiatrist, you know how it goes."

Carmichael nodded. "They'd never return her though, would they? I mean, return her to her mother?" she asked, remembering as she asked the question Mrs. Abbott's drinking from the whisky bottle. She wondered just how many people knew the woman drank.

"Hard to say. They never like to part mother and child, you know, not unless they have to. I suppose they're right, but about a year ago we had another kid brought in, Georgina. I remember that child. She was returned to her mother eventually and then brought in dead. Oh, I realize it's hard for the social workers to know what to do. It's a worry, isn't it?" She got up.

"Yes, it certainly is. Sister Jones will be upset," said Carmichael, and Miss Excell nodded.

"She's devoted to those children. Yes, she'll be upset.

She's tried to hold on to Marie, both times she's been in, but in the end . . . Well, I must go. Thanks again. Everything all right?"

Carmichael nodded. "Yes, thank you, Miss Excell. We're one nurse short, as you probably know, off sick. This morning there are only three clinics, so it's O.K. This afternoon, well, we shall be a bit pushed."

"I'll see what I can do. I'll send you a relief if I've got one. I'm not promising, though," said Miss Excell.

"I can manage," said Carmichael quickly. It didn't do to ask for staff, it was much better to "manage."

"See what I can do," said the Nursing Officer as a nurse poked her head round the office door, saying, "Sister, Dr. Ahmed wants an Esbach's bandage. We haven't got one, have we? I've only seen them in training school."

Sister Carmichael looked at Miss Excell, and Miss Excell raised her eyes to heaven. "They'll be asking for leeches next," she said. "If you can't find one, there's probably one in the splint room. No, don't bother to see me out, I'll make my own way. You've got enough to cope with," and she smiled and disappeared.

Carmichael turned to the nurse. "I'll come with you, nurse," she said. "I'll talk to Dr. Ahmed and see what he wants. If necessary, we'll have to search the splint room as Miss Excell suggests, but perhaps it's not really an Esbach he wants, sometimes the language difficulty . . ." The nurse nodded and Carmichael and she made their way down to the orthopaedic clinic where the Indian doctor was working.

20

Up in the operating theatre, little Marie Abbott was lying on the theatre table, anaesthetized, and for the moment happily oblivious to her various injuries. Before the green towel was put over her entire small form, the anaesthetist, gently placing a small anaesthetic face piece over the bruised mouth and nose, said cryptically, "Undernourished, as well."

The orthopaedic surgeon looked up at her. He had been watching the nurse snip the bandages that held the green dressing towel in place over Marie's injured left leg. "As well, Henrietta," he said to the anaesthetist. "As well, poor little devil. Saunderson's going to have a go at the eyelid, but I thought the compound had better be done first. After all, a three-year-old can be susceptible to gas gangrene or . . . The sooner it's closed, the better." The green towel was placed over Marie and obliterated her almost completely. The injured leg remained visible. The nurse folded back the green towel and looked up at the orthopaedic surgeon.

"M-m," he said, holding his gloved hands together and bending forward to get a good look at the injury. "Not as bad as I thought, really. The alignment, well, a little push should straighten it, reduce it, it's just a question of how much muscle and tissue injury there is."

"What of growth, sir?" asked Dr. Ahmed, the doctor who was assisting him.

"She may have one leg a little shorter than the other, if

nothing worse," the surgeon answered. His tone was tired, not because of the amount of work he'd done, but because it was a child, and anything like this happening to a child made everyone sad, particularly when there was a suspicion of . . .

"Anyway, off we go," he said, and Sister came over and stood by Dr. Ahmed, and the surgeon gently began to probe the injured leg, having looked at the anaesthetist to get a nod of assent for the start. Manipulating the small leg, he turned to the radiographer, clad in green like the rest of the theatre staff and standing beside her machine.

"Pictures, please," he said, and she wheeled the portable X-ray machine over to the theatre table and positioned it above Marie's leg. The nurse held out a sterile towel and the radiographer placed a cassette in it. Nurse deftly wrapped the large cassette, the surgeon and Dr. Ahmed lifted the leg, and the cassette was placed underneath. A whirr and a click, the picture was taken, again the leg lifted, the cassette removed, and the same thing done again once more with the leg turned slightly sideways. The radiographer, careful not to touch the nurse or any part of the sterile theatre table, took both cassettes and walked out of the theatre into the dark-room, and everybody waited.

The operation could not proceed until the orthopaedic surgeon had checked that his reduction was as good as it could be.

The theatre Sister, the orthopaedic surgeon, and the Indian registrar stood back from the table, waiting for the radiographer to bring the plates back. They were silent, looking at the small form on the theatre table, and then the anaesthetist spoke. "Who the hell would do a thing like this? It just beggars description, it's too much."

She took the mask off the small face and looked down at it. The battered eyes, split lip, the bruising; she gently put the mask back and looked at the surgeon.

"Not proven yet," he said brusquely. "Sometimes I think it seems a farce, or most of it. Case conferences, goodness knows what, while people make up their minds, and the child goes on suffering. Then . . . even then, they send the kid back to the mother. Well . . . I suppose that's not my end of the business. There's one thing, it's not often you see a compound fracture, not on a kid of this size. How the hell was it done? Falling down the stairs, they say. Some stairs, must have been made of steel plate."

"What about the wrist? Going to do it now, sir?" theatre Sister asked him.

"Might as well, it only needs a pull."

The surgeon looked over to the nurse who was looking after the plaster trolley and nodded to her. The nurse automatically opened some smaller plaster bandages and started making a slab for the small arm.

At that moment the door opened and the radiographer came back into the theatre. She held two X-ray plates in her hand. One she thrust up on to the X-ray screen. The surgeon walked over to it, his rubber-gloved hands clasped in front of him, and looked at the screen critically. "Could be better, but I don't know, there's a splinter of bone there. I think I'll leave it, though, it's close enough. Now let's look at the lateral."

The radiographer pulled the plate down from the screen and thrust up another, and the surgeon looked at that one.

"M-m, not so bad, the lateral position is quite good, really, alignment good, think we'll leave it. Sew it up." He turned round and nodded to the assistant. "O.K., we'll stitch up and plaster, I think it'll do. I don't think I'll get it any better messing about with it."

"It's not bad, not bad line—alignment position . . . ?" Dr. Ahmed said in his halting English, and the orthopaedic surgeon nodded.

"As I said, it's as good as I can get it. I don't think there's

any point in messing about with it any longer. We'll close."
The theatre Sister breathed softly in relief. Any more delay
and her list, already held up by this emergency, would be
going on far into the evening. The anaesthetist, too, looked
relieved.

"Come on then, sutures," said the surgeon, walking up
close to the table. Dr. Ahmed handed him a pair of forceps
in which was clamped a needle with a suture dangling from
it. The nurse with the plaster trolley imperceptibly began to
move forward at Sister's nod. The bowl of water attached to
the trolley slopped slightly as she did so, and the Sister
frowned; the nurse steadied it, then continued to push the
trolley gently forward. The suture needle went back and
forward in the flesh of the small leg, closing in a long, neat
wound.

"Did you meet the mother?" the anaesthetist asked.

"Yes, I did. I had a talk with her. Funny woman, I
thought, smelled of booze, but then somebody might have
given her brandy. She was cold, unmoved apparently, but
that might be shock, of course. After all, the woman's just
getting over the loss of her husband. I suppose we'd better
give her the benefit of the doubt."

Little Marie Abbott, oblivious to all this, anaesthetized,
later to wake to pain, but at the moment unconscious,
breathed steadily and quietly.

"Patient all right?" asked the surgeon, and the anaesthetist nodded reassuringly.

"O.K.," she said, "quite O.K."

21

A week went by fairly uneventfully, and Carmichael had only one incident which made the week, in a way, slightly memorable: a brush with Nurse Winter.

It was during the morning of the new arrangement regarding the ear, nose, and throat clinic and the psychiatric clinic. Nurse Winter had vanished in with the elderly psychiatrist and was showing signs of rebellion as she came out to the waiting-room phone to order coffee for him. She glanced at Carmichael, and Carmichael's eyes met hers. There was obvious belligerence in them, and when she ushered in the next patient to the psychiatrist, Nurse Winter, head in air, walked by Carmichael's office and down to the ear, nose, and throat clinic. It was a direct and open challenge. She was going to speak to her boy-friend, Dr. Easton. That clinic had paused for the coffee-break as well.

Carmichael sat quite still. What should she do? Should she go and tell the nurse to go back to her own clinic? There was no actual need for her to be in the psychiatric clinic at the moment, for he was lodged with a patient, and would be, probably, for the next twenty minutes. On the other hand, she should not leave her clinic, particularly to go in to Dr. Easton. Carmichael got up and decided to go and see what was happening. Sometimes the E.N.T. surgeon, Dr. Simm, and his clinical assistant got together over coffee and chatted about the cases. Sometimes Dr. Simm refused coffee altogether and went straight on with his patients, particularly if he was a little behind his appointment schedule. This morning exactly that had happened and Dr. Simm and his nurse were proceeding with the clinic. As Carmichael looked in and gave him a pleasant "Good morning," he did not move his head, his E.N.T. mirror light being focused firmly on the patient's ear. The patient's head was turned away to the window and the auriscope in the ear flashed as the light met the metal, but he answered amiably. "Good morning, Sister, right up to date, I think we are, eh, nurse?" The nurse looked at Sister and nodded.

Carmichael then moved forward to the next clinic. The door was shut and she could hear voices inside. Nurse Baker, at that moment, emerged from the room, closing the door ostentatiously behind her. She looked startled when she saw Carmichael. "Oh, Sister, I was just going to pop over to the pharmacy. Dr. Easton wants . . ." It was an obvious lie and Baker was not good at it; there was nothing needed from the pharmacy.

Sister Carmichael looked at her. "What you are trying to say is that Nurse Winter has asked you to leave her alone with Dr. Easton for a minute, Staff Nurse, isn't that so?" Carmichael's mouth twisted with a contemptuous look, and Baker nodded miserably.

"Well, they're . . . they do . . . they have . . ." She paused.

Sister Carmichael took her up sharply. "What they do, or they have, or they are, is of little interest to me in the middle of an ear, nose, and throat clinic. You will go back in, please, and send Nurse Winter to me." Carmichael stalked back to her office.

In about three minutes, a long time to the impatient Out Patients Sister, Winter walked into her office. "Yes, Sister?" she said, and her head was held high. "You wanted me, Staff Baker said."

"What are you doing out of your clinic, Nurse Winter?"

Carmichael asked, shuffling the papers on her desk, and not looking up at the girl in front of her. She didn't want to see the pretty, indignant face, the large grey eyes, the long, turned-up lashes, the mouth that was red and full-lipped and beautifully shaped even without lipstick.

"I just went to speak to Dr. Easton; the psychiatrist is perfectly all right, I left him with a patient."

"You don't know what the psychiatrist might ask for," said Carmichael coldly. "In any case I do not like the clinic being left."

"All right, Sister, I'm sorry; but I wish you hadn't taken me off Dr. Easton's clinic, and I can't think why you did. I ran it . . . I ran it properly; and now, well, I used to like Out Patients, but I don't now. I hate it since you've come. When Staff Newman was here it was different, it was nice, and now well, it's so tense and . . ."

"More efficient, perhaps," Sister Carmichael threw in.

"No, not more efficient, Sister, the doctors are not as happy as they were in the department. You can say what you like, and I don't care if you report me to the Nursing Officer. It's true, the place is not as, well . . . contented, and I believe that the patients can sense that, too."

"You are referring, of course, to Dr. Easton," said Carmichael, looking up sharply, but her face was receptive.

"No, I'm not, I'm referring to all of them. Even the surgeons, the orthopaedic men, one of them said the other day that the atmosphere was electric in this department, whereas it used to be very nice and relaxed."

"Very relaxed, from all I hear," said Carmichael.

"I don't know what you mean by that, Sister, but if you're making nasty remarks about Newman, I don't like it. She was a friend of mine, even though she was acting Sister. She was a good scout, I liked her, and the department was better then." Quite suddenly Winter burst into tears.

"Sit down, nurse. Surely this can't be springing merely

from my changing your clinic. What is it?" Carmichael said, her tone slightly less acid.

"Well, we had a row, Dr. Easton and I, on our last date. You wouldn't understand, you wouldn't understand at all, but I was going to try to put it right, that's all, that's why I went down there, but it's no good, Sister Carmichael. If I'd asked acting Sister Newman, she'd have understood. She'd have said, well, go and have a word with him, but don't be long, and gone in and looked after the psychiatric clinic herself. She was like that, but you wouldn't understand, you'd think that was incompetent, and inefficient, I suppose."

"Well, I suggest you go in and see the psychiatrist now, his coffee has just gone in, and his patient has just come out. Perhaps the coffee with him will make you feel better." Carmichael's voice was still prim, and yet not quite so cold.

Winter got up, took a handkerchief from her apron bib and wiped her eyes. "I'm sorry if what I've said has made you cross, but I can't take back a thing, Sister, it's true," she said and beat a hasty retreat.

Carmichael sat, gazing at her desk blotter, and then with a pen started to doodle on the white blotting pad, which had been put in fresh this morning by one of the nurses. If they had done such a thing she would have been furious, wasting good blotting paper, but somehow Winter had given her something to think about. Was it true? Did the men say that? She had tried to be efficient; she was proud of this job. After all, she'd been the one to get it. Admittedly there hadn't been very many people for the appointment, but she'd got it. Why? Because of her confidence, the confidence born of . . . She looked at the blotter; she had written in large, ornate letters "M.H." Marion Hughes, the woman who, in her last hospital, had driven her so many times to despair. She made a smaller doodle "M.H." She mustn't get like that. She had hated Marion Hughes and so had everyone else in the hospital. No, she mustn't get like that. She wanted to be . . . not popular, but well liked. Thought efficient, by the doctors particularly. She looked along at the closed door of the psychiatric clinic. She wondered if Winter was talking about her, and shook her head. No. Anyway, Carmichael felt her heart lift a little. Miss Excell, the Nursing Officer, liked her; that was something. But was it true, had she altered the department? God knows, Marion Hughes had altered the hospital. She must guard against it, she mustn't be like that. Nothing, nothing, must make this job anything but a success. She must still be efficient, still be distant, but there was no need to be like M.H.

Suddenly she decided that next week she'd put Winter back to Dr. Easton's clinic and Baker back into the psychiatrist's. She took the pen more firmly between her thumb and forefinger, and scored out the letters "M.H." so heavily that the tip of the ballpoint went through the blotting paper and tore it. Carmichael hastily withdrew the paper, tore it up, threw it in the wastepaper basket, and put in a fresh piece. She got to her feet restlessly, walked across the waiting-room, smiling at one or two of the patients and asking them how they were. They nodded and replied, pleased. Yes, she must be careful; nothing, nothing, must come between her and the next step, Nursing Officer. After all, there might be something in what Winter said. Winter was young, but she understood men and that was more than Carmichael ever had.

The rest of the week went more serenely, and although Carmichael made a big effort, it was difficult for her. She felt the difficulty of the pleasant smile, of the pleasant remark. If the nurses noticed, it, they said nothing, or Carmichael heard nothing. She often caught scraps of conversation from the clinic room.

Friday came and there was a slight air of festivity; the

following Monday was a Bank Holiday, and that meant that nurses in the department would get an added day on their weekend. The wards would get a day, in lieu, later. Carmichael thought of the three days ahead of her: Saturday, Sunday, Monday. What should she do? It would be lonely. Of course, there was the Mini. She would, perhaps, make a little tour round, but before that there was her favourite clinic this afternoon, the neurologist's. He, Dr. Gregson, was a quick-tempered, hasty little man, who rushed through his clinic. Carmichael always took it. She had heard that Holly Newman, during the time she was acting Sister, had always taken the neurologist, because he frightened the nurses to death with his wish for speed.

"Don't let the patient's chair get warm, or they'll have sat there too long," was one of the first things he had said to Carmichael, and she had been rather shocked. Later, in his clinics, she had come to admire him. Come to admire the way that he might hurry the history, but never skimp the examination, and he never missed anything. Indeed, he was one of the leading neurologists in England. He'd once said to her during the time she had been taking his clinic, "I like the way you have reorganized my clinic, Sister, well done. We get through it quicker, get home sooner, the patient is satisfied, so am I, and I expect you are too. Right?" He had hardly waited for her to reply, but Carmichael had felt an unaccustomed glow of pleasure. She had not had much praise during her nursing career, indeed during her life, so it came pleasantly to her.

She had said, "Oh, thank you, Dr. Gregson, I do my best." His reply, "And it's a good best, too, Sister," had pleased her further. This afternoon's clinic followed this pleasant pattern.

Now she remembered this, she thought again of Winter and something she could do to make the weekend more pleasant for her; so, as she saw the girl repassing her office, she called out, "Nurse Winter."

The nurse paused and looked at her, half apprehensively and half with hostility. "Yes, Sister Carmichael," she said, and came up to the office door.

"I think next week we'll go back to the usual routine; you can take Dr. Easton's clinic and we'll put Nurse Baker back with the psychiatrist. I expect she's learned quite a bit about ear, nose, and throat."

There was a pause. Nurse Winter looked curiously at Carmichael, then dropped her eyes and said demurely, "Thank you very much, Sister Carmichael, that's very nice of you, I shall be glad to get back. I don't find the psychiatrist terribly interesting, but I won't . . . I won't take advantage."

"Well, perhaps Nurse Baker doesn't find the psychiatrist very interesting either, but I believe she prefers him to Dr. Easton." It was a parting shot that Carmichael couldn't resist, but Winter was too pleased to worry about it.

"I hope you have a nice weekend, Sister. Are you going away?" she asked.

Carmichael shook her head. "No, I'm not going away, but I shall probably tour round in my car." The pride with which she said it was obvious, but Winter no longer felt the desire to giggle at the way Carmichael's weekend was to be spent.

"Have a really nice time, Sister," she said, and her tone was warm. Carmichael felt better for it. She mustn't fall into the trap that Marion Hughes had fallen into, oh no, she mustn't do that. She didn't want anyone to feel like getting rid of her. It was nice to be liked, not too much, and not at the expense of discipline, of course, but it was nice to be liked. Carmichael got up, closed the drawer of her desk, tidied the top, and picked her handbag up from the side of her desk where she had placed it ready to go, before she decided to speak to Winter.

At that moment Nurse Baker put her head round the door. "Hope you have a nice weekend, Sister," she said.

Carmichael nodded briefly. "Everybody gone?" she asked.

"Just Winter and I, but we've finished. Good night, Sister."

Sister Carmichael looked at her watch: twenty past five. She went and closed the front door of the department, pushed up the bolts. There was still someone in the records office; the glass partition was still open, and she called, "Good night, Miss Roberts."

The astonished Miss Roberts turned. "Good night, Sister Carmichael, have a nice weekend; nice to get Monday, isn't it?" she said.

"Yes, it is, very nice," replied Carmichael, and took herself off through the department with an unaccustomed glow, caused, she felt, by not being like Marion Hughes.

22

Saturday passed much as usual with Carmichael. She enjoyed getting up late, morning tea, a leisurely breakfast, shopping, cleaning, dusting the car, lunch; then in the late afternoon, sitting down in front of the black and white television. She was already contemplating getting a colour set.

On Sunday, when she woke, the sun was shining in the bedroom and the sky was blue. She was pleased she had decided to take herself on a picnic and knew exactly where she was going, about fifteen miles away, up a long road that led to the top of the hills, which gave a beautiful view of the valley below surrounded by green, lush hills. Here Carmichael wanted to sit and have her picnic, read her book, and enjoy her afternoon in the sunshine.

She cut sandwiches, put them in a plastic box she kept specially for this purpose, filled the thermos flask with coffee, got a cardigan out of her bedroom drawer, just in case she should get chilly, collected her new historical novel and handbag, closed her front door, and went down to the garages.

Four of the garage doors were open, and the cars gone, three were shut. When she had opened hers, she remembered it was a Bank Holiday tomorrow, an extra day. She wasn't used to having a Bank Holiday off; she'd always worked on a ward, not in an Out Patients department before. She had usually had to have the day in lieu like the rest of them, and she had got used to it.

She backed the car out, and set off to the spot she had in mind. When she got there, she was pleasantly surprised. There was no other car in the lay-by; she had expected at least one or two, but this was good, to be alone on this lovely hillside; to be able to look down at the beautiful valley divided into fields of gold, green and brown, in solitude, was lovely.

She got out of the car and stood there a moment, deciding where to spread her rug. There, under the tree; the sun was hot, and the tree would give just that little bit of shade to enable her to read in comfort.

Way across the valley, she could see diminutive black and white cows; a bird soared across the valley—it was beautiful. As she watched, the shadow of a small cloud scudded across the valley, making a moving shadow. Carmichael knew this spot; she'd been here once before and liked it. This morning she liked it even more.

She settled herself on the car rug, with her belongings around her, stretching her feet and legs out into the warm sunshine, deciding to have a cup of coffee now, and poured one from the steaming thermos, corking it, and putting it back beside her. This was really something to enjoy. She looked around her. The air smelled so good, and for once there was no sign of her hay fever. She turned on her side on the rug and opened her book, but her eyes were drawn back again to the view; it was so lovely, so quiet. She heard a dog barking from a farm somewhere, and looked around but could see no sign of habitation. Now and again a car passed on the road behind the Mini, but not many. It was not a main road, but on the way she had met a stream of traffic going, she presumed, south to the coast. Thank goodness she wasn't in its slow-moving stream; she was happier up here alone.

She read for about half an hour, then her peace was suddenly shattered. Another car drew in beside the Mini, and five people—three adults, two children, and a dog—spewed out. The adults argued as to where they should sit, the children ran about squealing, and the dog barked. Carmichael turned her back on them and tried to ignore them, but the big black dog rushed up to her, wagging its tail, and before she could stop it, picked up her cardigan and ran away with it.

"Mum, Dad, Jason's pinched the lady's woolly—I'll catch him," one of the children yelled. He dashed after the dog, who by this time was dragging the cardigan across the grass. Soon the whole family was in pursuit. Then, having got the woolly away from Jason, the woman, presumably the mother of the two children, brought it back to Carmichael, brushing off the dog's saliva with her hand.

"I'm so sorry," she said. "It's only that he likes to bring a present. He's a retriever, you see." Her eyes, apologetic yet humorous, met Carmichael's stony stare.

Carmichael's voice was clipped with annoyance. "You should keep the dog under better control," she said, and turned away.

The man, standing awkwardly behind the woman, said, "I think we'd better try somewhere else, dear," and the woman nodded.

They all piled back into the car; the dog, his head hanging out of the back window, appeared to give Carmichael a parting grin. She picked up the cardigan, a look of annoyance on her face, folding the damp part, where the dog's mouth had held it, inside, and put it back beside her.

At a quarter to one she ate her sandwiches and drank her coffee. They were not as enjoyable as she had hoped, but the sun continued to shine, and Carmichael turned once again to her book but couldn't concentrate on it, and her eyes once again turned to the valley.

Suddenly they focused on something bright yellow on the right side of the hill. Carmichael leaned forward to see more clearly, pushing her glasses back up her nose. It was a hang-glider; she saw it launch itself out into space and glide across the valley, turning again slightly higher, then slightly lower, dipping, weaving, quite beautiful. Yet for some reason it filled Carmichael with depression and a terrible feeling of loneliness. She watched the man in the glider; he was so sure of himself, so perfect in his control of the great wings. It occurred to her that he would go home and tell his wife, or girl-friend, all about his flight, how long he'd been in the air; or perhaps his mother or man friend. At that moment another glider she hadn't noticed, on the other side of the hill, launched itself off over the valley. This time it was a blue one. She watched the two of them, soaring about, and thought with bitterness—there would be two.

This feeling of loneliness was alien to Carmichael. At St. Jude's there'd been so much to worry about, so much to battle with, there hadn't been time for loneliness; even when she'd got home she'd been worrying about Marion Hughes, about what she'd done on the ward, and the tears, too, she'd shed—well, they'd taken up the time. Now she had so much; she'd fought for it and got it. But who to tell about it?

Then, look what she'd done at St. Jude's. And here, there was Marie Abbott . . . She shook her head almost savagely; she would love to tell someone. To be able to go home to her flat and say, "Well, I finished him." But she couldn't. You can't say you've killed someone to a friend or to a relative, no matter how proud you are, you just can't say it. No, that was something she would have to keep to herself for ever. Of course, one could have a companion and not tell them, but that just wouldn't be worth it.

She thought of her nurses and colleagues; Winter, Baker, Miss Excell, Jones, they all had someone. Jones had an old mother, Winter probably was out with Dr. Easton, Baker had a sister. Even that awful Philip Marks, he had a girl-friend, one of the nurses chasing him; the way these girls chased men! But wasn't that just so that they wouldn't be lonely, wouldn't land up like her, looking down on a valley, alone?

Carmichael felt she couldn't stand another moment here. The hang-gliders had disappeared, but as she stood up and started to fold up her car rug and collect her things, she saw them, down in the valley. They had landed and were talking to each other. You see, she said to herself, everybody's got somebody, or so it seems; but there must be other lonely people in the world—I'm just being stupid. But she couldn't dispel the depression. As if to match her mood, a large cloud came across the sun and plunged the valley into momentary shade. It was followed by other clouds. Carmichael shivered, picked up her things, put them in the Mini, got in, and sat with her hands on the steering wheel. No one knows I'm here, or cares, she thought. Even in the luxury and familiar joy of her small car, the feeling didn't go. Even seated with her hands on the steering wheel, which was usually where she felt so happy, no.

She turned the car and drove home slowly. She found she was talking to herself, and looked round guiltily, as if there was someone to hear her, she thought, and again she thought of Marion Hughes, and Major Abbott.

What a beastly thing to do to a child. I wouldn't have done that even when they irritated me to death on the children's ward; I would never dream of even smacking a child. He deserved death. Then the Mini . . .

At home, the kettle that she put on to make the tea clicked. She poured water into the teapot and took her tray through to the sitting-room. She switched on the television, but it was showing an old gangster film, and so she turned it off. The silence of the flat was oppressive. She felt as if someone were listening as well as herself, an odd feeling. She counted her blessings; she was a Sister now with a nice flat, a nice car, but all this fell quite flat and did nothing to lift her.

Tomorrow was Monday, another blank day; she wouldn't go up there again. Well, let tomorrow take care of itself for the moment, but she wished, how she wished she was going to work, wished she was going to sit in her office, oversee the department, feel secure. But she wasn't. This evening she'd go to the pictures. She picked up the local paper and thumbed through it. There was nothing much she wanted to see but a horror film. Well, that might take her mind off herself; she decided to go. The only sound in the flat was the ticking of the clock. She had again this strange feeling that she and someone beside her were listening to it. It was a strange, strange feeling.

She slipped on a light coat, picked up her handbag, checked the paper again for the name of the picture house to which she was going, and closed her front door firmly behind her. The feeling that she had someone else beside her, listening, that she had experienced in the flat, disappeared. She held her head high again and walked down the stairs. She was Sister Carmichael going to the movies.

23

When Carmichael woke on Monday, the Bank Holiday morning, she kept her eyes closed for a moment or two to try and assess how she felt, to see whether yesterday's depression, apprehension, fear, was still there. After a little she felt it was much the same as yesterday. She hadn't been able to sit through the horror movie, but had left and come home, again to depression. It had only really lifted once after seeing the hang-gliders; why on earth had that precipitated it? She moved her head restlessly on the pillow, and remembered. The only time the depression had lifted was on the way home as she had passed Millstream House; yes, she had felt better then. But by the time she had got home, the depression had been back again. She opened her eyes and gazed at her window. No blue sky, just dull, grey clouds. A gust of wind blew against the glass pane—a nasty day, a typical English Bank Holiday day. So many people would be saying that. Carmichael moved her head restlessly on the pillow. There was no pleasure in being in the flat today.

Was it the need to tell someone that had made her feel as she did yesterday? Well, that was stupid—to tell somebody that you'd killed was not exactly a sensible conversation; it wouldn't do you any good, or them, or the person who was dead. With an impatient jerk she got up, swung her legs out of bed, went over to the window, and looked out through the rain-drenched glass.

What should she do today? She turned from the window,

shrugged into her dressing-gown, made her tea, and brought it back to bed. After she'd finished her tea, she got up again and went out into the hall; no newspaper. Sometimes there seemed to be a paper on Bank Holidays, sometimes not. This morning, by the look of it, there was not.

Well, one thing she was decided upon: she was not taking the Mini out, not in this weather; she didn't like getting it wet. Even if you dried it off when you got back and put it in the garage, the underneath would still be wet and that's how the rust started. No, it was better where it was, safe away from the weather.

Anyhow, there were the usual things to be done in the flat, and she'd got some knitting she could do. This Bank Holiday business, she'd have to get used to it now she was Out Patients Sister. Well, she'd got her lunch, that was pleasant—pork chops. They would make a nice meal.

She ran herself a bath, and while she was lying in the foamy water, she suddenly had an idea: why not ask Sister Jones to tea? After all, it would be rather pleasant. She'd only got biscuits, and didn't know that she was up to making a cake; she'd never really been one for making cakes or buns. No, she'd ask her to tea and say on the phone she'd only got biscuits. Jones would put up with it. Perhaps she'd come. She thought she remembered her saying she'd got a half day, but maybe she was wrong; anyway, she'd try.

After her bath she pottered around with a duster for about an hour and repolished the little table that she'd picked up cheaply in the sale-room because she thought it was pretty. The phone stood on it. She stepped back and looked at it admiringly and then went into the sitting-room and looked at the clock—ten o'clock. She'd make herself some coffee and then phone Jones.

"May I speak to the children's ward, please?" The switchboard operator put her through promptly.

"Yes?" A nurse on the other end answered the phone,

and Carmichael made a mental note to tell Sister Jones that there was a certain nurse, she didn't know who, on the ward who didn't know how to answer the phone properly. Even as the thought came to her, she dismissed it, thinking that is exactly what Marion Hughes would have done.

"It's Sister Carmichael, nurse, can I speak to Sister Jones?"

Immediately the tone of voice at the other end altered. "Oh, yes, Sister Carmichael, just hang on and I'll fetch her, I won't be a minute." There was a crash as the nurse put the phone heavily down on Sister's desk. Carmichael shook her head and waited. She could hear the noises of the ward: a child crying, a trolley clattering past Sister's office door, a nurse calling out to another. Carmichael wished she was there.

"Yes, hallo, Carmichael, that you, lucky old thing to be off duty." It was Jones' cheerful voice.

"Yes, I just rang up to see if you would like to come to tea this afternoon, I believe you said you'd got a half day? I know you've seen the flat, but I thought you might like to see what I've done to it, would you?" Carmichael ended on a rather hesitant note.

"Yes, I'd like that, if you could make it about half past three. I've got to go out at six tonight, and need to be back to put on my glad rags by about half past five. Would that be O.K.?"

"Yes, I've only got biscuits, I haven't got any cake, I just asked you on the spur of the moment," Carmichael finished lamely, but Jones sounded quite happy.

"O.K. See you at three-thirty. Look forward to it, busy now. 'Bye." The phone went down at the other end and Carmichael stood for a moment in the hall. That was nice; it would be something to look forward to. She would get her tea-set out, at least the half tea-set that they'd given her when she left St. Jude's. It was pretty; she'd felt a bit let down when she'd seen what a small present she'd got, but now she was pleased that she'd got it. Yes, and she'd got some paper doilies; she'd put one out for the biscuits, and those little napkins that that child's mother had given her. At the time, she'd looked at them and thought, Just an unwanted Christmas present, but again she was glad of them now and felt a bit ashamed at the way she'd received them.

She began to bustle about, feeling that there was something in the day now, something going to happen, someone whom she could talk to. It was almost certain that Jones would talk shop, but no matter. What else was there really for them to talk about? They knew nothing of each other outside the hospital.

Jones had a date tonight. Well, Carmichael would pretend that she had a date, too. She would say she was going out to dinner, maybe. Perhaps to someone's house, not a restaurant; that way you could be tripped up, for someone might say, "You've been there, haven't you, you went there last Bank Holiday, what was it like?" Liars must have good memories.

A face flashed in front of her, a face with hard brown eyes, grey hair swept back into a stern Eton crop, a straight mouth. What had she done? She must have been perhaps five at the time. Why should she remember that now? She smiled grimly to herself. What was it? Some small lie she'd told to get out of trouble, some small misdemeanour? Well, at least the remark that she hadn't understood at the time had come in useful now.

The morning wore on, and the rain didn't stop; it looked as though it had been raining and was going to rain for ever. The leaden skies, the drenched trees were hardly stimulating. Carmichael switched on the television, though she didn't like sport. It was worth having it on; the noise, the picture, were companionable. She ate her lunch in front of it, and because Jones—someone—was coming, she enjoyed her lunch more, and pushed aside, almost completely, but not quite, yesterday's strange feeling.

Towards three-thirty, Carmichael began to move restlessly around the flat. She'd washed up her lunch things, cleared everything away, laid the tray with her new tea-set; it was the first time it had been used, and the tray looked really nice. She went into her sitting-room and put the table ready by the settee, then looked out of the window again. No one there. She went back into the bedroom and for the third time smoothed the coverlet of her bed, then back to the window. At last.

Jones' old car drew up outside. She saw the door open and Jones' legs swing out, then saw her struggle rather laboriously out of the car. The driver's side was on the camber of the road and made it, for anyone of Jones' build, rather difficult to get out, whereas Carmichael, lithe and slim, had no difficulty. She let the curtain drop back into place, went into the kitchen, emptied the kettle, put more water in, and switched it on. By the time she'd done that, her front doorbell was ringing, and she went and opened the door.

"For God's sake, these stairs, glad we haven't got them in our house, be too much for me, I've really got to slim. Thank God, you haven't got any cream cakes, I should eat them." Jones came in on this remark, laughing and taking off her coat at the same time. "It's not wet, just a few drops when I got out of the car. Where shall I put it?"

Carmichael took it from her and hung it up on some hooks she'd had put in the hall when she came. She took Sister Jones' scarf and hung that up as well. Then they went through into the sitting-room.

"Golly, you've certainly done yourself well," said Jones, looking round admiringly. "This room really looks nicer than when Holly had it. I love the settee and the chairs; lovely colour green."

Carmichael nodded. "Dawn green, it's called," she said.

Jones flopped down on the sofa. "M-m, a bit hard though," she said. "I like these old-fashioned settees, you know, very low, that you can lie down on and watch television, curl your feet up. These you have to sit up proper, neat, and tidy, as my grandmother used to say." She laughed again.

"I like to sit up straight, we were always encouraged to as children, I suppose that's why I still do," answered Carmichael.

"Well, my Mum and Dad were pretty easy-going, we flopped about quite a bit, that's why I do now. Were your father and mother strict, then?" said Jones easily.

Carmichael looked at her but did not answer. There was a click and, almost with relief, Carmichael turned away. "I'll make the tea," she said, and disappeared to the kitchen. Jones nodded to herself and looked round the room again.

As Carmichael came in with the tray of tea and put it on the table beside the settee, she said, "We'll wait a minute, shall we, and let it brew a bit. You like strong tea, don't you?"

Jones nodded. "Yes," she said absently. "By the way, I see you bought Holly's carpets and curtains, that was sensible of you."

"Yes, I would have liked everything new, but that would have been pretty pricey, what with the flat and the new Mini, so I decided to have them. Well, they go quite well, don't they?"

Jones nodded. "They certainly do. I think the whole flat's nice. While the tea's brewing, can I have a look round?"

Carmichael had really wanted to give her a guided tour herself, but Jones poked her head in the bathroom and remarked, "H-m, new glass shelf, and a new bathroom cupboard—nice." In the bedroom she said, "I like that," when she looked at Carmichael's bed with the much-smoothed cover, and the light wood furniture. "I'd like that, I'd like that very much, but I can't afford it, so it's no use wanting. I think you've got the flat jolly nice, I really do. You'll have some fun up here, I reckon."

"Yes," Carmichael nodded; she was not going to tell Jones that she was her first visitor. She started to put milk in the cups.

"What a pretty tea service. Did you buy that when you came in, too?" asked Jones.

"No, they gave me this when I left St. Jude's, and the . . ." She stopped; she was going to say "the tea-napkins" but Jones had already taken one, screwed it up, and put it on the settee beside her. Obviously Jones was above such things as tea-napkins, so Carmichael said nothing.

The atmosphere became a little flat as both women sought to find common ground, which, of course, was the hospital.

"Winter and Dr. Easton may make a go of it then," said Jones. "I believe they're going to get engaged."

"Oh, really?" said Carmichael without much interest.

"Little Marie, you know Marie Abbott, she's better, had her drip taken down today. Poor little bugger. Hope that second case conference goes well. I mean, if they let her go home to her mother . . . They do their best, but they don't seem to have much power, I dunno."

"Has her mother been to see her?" Carmichael asked, pouring Jones another cup of tea.

"Yeah, she came yesterday. I watched, I wanted to see the kid's reaction. She didn't turn away from her mother, that I'll admit, but how could you tell? I mean, poor little sod; well, she had one arm in a splint with a drip, the other in plaster because she's got a green-stick fracture of her wrist, a leg on traction and both eyes half-closed. I mean, you can't expect to get much reaction from a poor little devil like that, can you? She's talking though—not prattling like the others, but at least she's talking. I didn't know what to make of the mother, though, she reeked of drink, looked awful, didn't stay long, I can't make head or tail of that woman." She took a sip of her fresh cup of tea, and put it down and reached for a biscuit.

"Oh, by the way, Mrs. Abbott asked your name."

"Asked my name? How could she? She doesn't know me," said Carmichael, turning her head sharply towards Jones.

"Well, she did. She said, who was the Sister who was in Casualty with the cut finger when she brought Marie in? You did something for her, about a bag, or something, forgotten what."

"Oh-h . . . A nurse had taken her up to the rest-room, and she left her handbag behind in Casualty. They were very busy so I took it up to her, that's all I did," answered Carmichael.

"Well, that's what it must have been then. She wanted to know who you were, I suppose as you'd done that for her . . ." Carmichael did not mention the whisky, the fact that she had reopened the door and seen Mrs. Abbott drinking out of the bottle. These things were best kept to oneself, and anyway, Jones would have made much of it, spread it about the hospital, and Carmichael didn't want that. What you knew and kept quiet about was still yours to use if you wished.

During the rest of the time Carmichael learned quite a few of the hospital titbits of gossip. That Mr. Simm, the elderly E.N.T. surgeon, was not above a bit of slap and tickle with the younger nurses, especially at the hospital dance; that Stuart Martin was having an affair with the Sister on the women's surgical ward; that the men's surgical ward Sister was reckoned to be a lez and was leaving to be with her friend in the north country. One of the male Staff Nurses was being promoted to her job, and some said that Mrs. Wright, one of the Nursing Officers, was going to have a baby. All of these things Jones poured out as she ate most of the biscuits.

The clock on the mantelpiece ticked on, the room grew warm and cosy, and Carmichael felt better and almost dreaded the moment when Jones would go. It was twenty-five past five when Jones eventually looked at the clock. "Golly, I'd better be going. Has it stopped raining?" She got up and went across the room and looked out of the window. "No, it's still pouring down, and I'm driving tonight. I hate driving in the wet and dark, don't you?"

Carmichael nodded. "I'm going out tonight, but I'm being called for," she said.

"Oh, bully for you; I always seem to have to do the ferrying, I dunno why. Who are you going out with—anyone I know?" asked Jones.

"I don't think so." There was a primness in Carmichael's voice that made Jones smile.

"All right, keep it dark, don't tell me if you don't want to," she said, and made her way into the hall. Carmichael held out her coat for her, then Jones took the scarf off the hook herself and tied it round her hair.

"Had me hair done Saturday, doesn't make much difference, but I don't want to get the little set there is in it wet, do I?" She tied the scarf under her chin. "Thanks for the tea, it was nice to see the flat, you must come round and see me and Mum sometime."

Carmichael nodded and opened the front door for her. She had a sudden rush of these strange feelings of apprehension at being alone again.

"Ta ta, then, be seeing you tomorrow, I expect," and Jones walked through Carmichael's front door and started down the stairs, turning round and waving her hand as she did so.

"Goodbye, and thanks for coming," said Carmichael automatically, then closed the door.

She washed up the cups and saucers, put the few remaining biscuits back in the tin, and stood the tray back on the working surface. The silence of the flat was again oppressive. The feeling of fear rushed in on her again. Fear of what? She turned on the television; she was better with noise. The Bank Holiday seemed to have made the street deserted, no cars going by, just the rain silently pouring down. At that moment the telephone rang.

Carmichael jumped, then steadied herself—a wrong number obviously. Who would ring her? There was no one to ring her. When she'd taken the flat, she'd wondered whether she should keep on Holly Newman's phone, and decided, yes, Sisters had telephones. This was the first time it had rung.

She walked through into the little hall and looked down at the cream telephone on the newly polished table. The phone went on ringing, and she picked up the receiver and put it to her ear. "Sister—er—I mean Miss Carmichael speaking," she said.

"Oh, Miss Carmichael speaking, is it, this is Christine Abbott." The voice at the other end of the phone sounded slurred. Carmichael thought, She's drunk. The voice went on.

"Did you hear? This is Christine Abbott speaking."

"Yes, Mrs. Abbott, what can I do for you?" Carmichael's voice was crisp.

"You can, perhaps, do some'n for me, but I can do a lot for you." The slurring voice went on, ending with a giggle.

"I see. Well, what, at the moment, do you wish me to do for you?"

"I want you to come round, it's only two streets away, I'll

give the address to you. Have you got a pencil?" A pad and pencil lay methodically beside the phone, but Carmichael felt she didn't need to write it down; once the woman said it, she'd remember.

"It's only two streets away from you, so you don't have to bring your Mini. Walk round, straight away if you can. I bet you're on your own, aren't you?" Mrs. Abbott went on after she'd given the address. Carmichael felt a flush creeping up her face.

"Very well, I'll come round now," she said.

"Alrigh', alrigh', I'll see you," said Mrs. Abbott, and the phone went down with a crash at the other end. Carmichael put hers down more gently.

How did Mrs. Abbott know she'd got a Mini? Carmichael thought, She couldn't possibly know, she hadn't recognized the car when Major Abbott backed into it, she hadn't even turned round, not even looked in her direction. No . . . What did she want to see her about? Well, it would be interesting to find out.

She went into the sitting-room to collect her handbag, and into the hall, slipped on a mac, took a rain hat out of the pocket and put it on. She checked to see that her keys were in her handbag. She certainly wouldn't take the Mini, but how . . . ? Well, it was no use wondering; she'd walk round and find out.

She walked down the stairs and started out into the rainy night. Why go? Why answer a drunken woman like Mrs. Abbott? Somehow, she felt she had to. At the back of her mind there was a fear, a fear of something; whatever Mrs. Abbott wanted, it had to be dealt with. Carmichael strode along the street firmly, in the pouring rain, taking no notice of it, towards Surbiton Grove.

24

As Carmichael walked through the rain, she felt slightly confused as to why she had answered Mrs. Abbott's summons so quickly. Perhaps the mention of the Mini, and the curiosity as to how Mrs. Abbott had known about it, was one of the things, but not altogether. She felt drawn towards the woman, drawn towards her in a strange, compelling way. She walked along, her flat shoes splashing in the puddles. She turned into Surbiton Grove.

The effect of the road, even on such a wet evening, was much the same on Carmichael as on Miss Grant, the social worker. Opulent, she thought, the neat lawns now drenched, the dripping shrubs, in spite of the wetness of the evening, it still looked rich. The dripping flowers— Carmichael could visualize them in the sunlight.

She walked on, looking at the name of each house, until she came to The Laburnums. She paused at the foot of the drive and looked up at the house. In spite of the fact that it was still daylight, there was a light shining through the panes of glass at the top of the front door. Carmichael stood there for a few seconds and was overwhelmed by the feeling that she would like to turn back, forget it, go away, but she couldn't. She walked on up the drive, her feet crunching on the gravel, less wet underfoot. She arrived at the front door and stepped up on to the one step, which was sheltered by an overhanging porch set above the front door. She pulled the cast-iron bell handle; the clang reverberated somewhere in the house; that was all. For a few moments she thought no one was going to answer and felt flooded with relief. Then she heard movement, and shortly after, a shadow appeared on the glass at the top of the door and the door opened.

Christine Abbott stood there, much as Carmichael had remembered her. Her fair hair was now slightly disarranged, as if she had been lying down, perhaps resting. She had on a blue dress, pale blue, the kind of colour one would associate with Mrs. Abbott, thought Carmichael. The neck was deeply cut and revealed her collar bones. She put out her hand to Carmichael in a vague gesture and said, "Sister Carmichael, yes, come in."

As she spoke, Carmichael smelled again the whisky on her breath, but Christine Abbott turned round and walked fairly steadily, but only fairly, across the parquet floor of the hall, her footsteps resounding on it as she crossed, avoiding the rugs as if she were afraid they might prove a hazard to her. She had left the front door open. Carmichael shut it quietly and followed Christine Abbott through into the sitting-room, noting as Miss Grant had done the furniture and luxury of the hall itself.

In the sitting-room Mrs. Abbott sank rather heavily on to the settee. Carmichael remained standing in her wet mackintosh and wetter headscarf. She said nothing and Christine Abbott struggled to her feet.

"Oh-h, I'm a rotten hostess, always have been. Charles is always saying . . . was always saying . . . that I'm a rotten hostess. It's true. Let me take your coat and that scarf." Carmichael slipped out of the mac and took off her scarf.

"It's wet, Mrs. Abbott," she said, and her voice was crisp.

"I can see that, I can see that . . . Just a minute and I'll put it in the cloakroom." She disappeared through the sitting-room door, and Carmichael remained standing. Within seconds Christine Abbott was back, and this time as she came through the door, she staggered just a little and held on to the lintel for a moment. She looked at Carmichael and laughed. "Will you have a drink? You'll probably need it." She picked up the empty glass which was standing on the table in front of the settee where she had been sitting and motioned to Carmichael to sit down. Carmichael tried to sit on the edge of the armchair to which Christine Abbott had motioned, but it was difficult. The soft, spongy cushion was not geared to letting people sit on the edge, so Carmichael moved back, not to be more comfortable, but to keep her balance.

"That's it, make yourself comfortable, it's a very comfortable chair, don't you think? It's a new suite Charles bought, just before he died, ready to go to the new house, which we're not going to now. Whisky, sherry, gin?" She leaned on the bar cart and looked towards Carmichael.

"No, thank you. I really don't drink . . ." Before she could finish the sentence, Mrs. Abbott broke in.

"Oh, God. Can't bear people who don't drink. Have something. Have a tomato juice?" Carmichael shook her head.

"No, thank you," she said firmly. Mrs. Abbott brought back her glass, a liberal supply of whisky in it, to which, Carmichael noticed, she had added neither soda nor water, merely dropped in an ice cube from the bucket standing on the bar top. She brought the glass over to the settee and sank down, drinking from the glass before she put it down on the table in front of her.

"Well, I expect, Sister Carmichael, you are wondering why I asked you here, isn't that so?" Christine Abbott took another drink from the glass, coughed slightly, and put it down again.

"Yes, I am," said Carmichael.

Christine Abbott opened a silver cigarette-box on the table beside her and offered it to Carmichael. "Cigarette?" The box wavered slightly in her hand, and her eyes drooped a little as she looked at Carmichael, and Carmichael noticed that the make-up on the eyelids was caked, the lids crêpey. Mrs. Abbott took a cigarette from the box although there was one already burning in the ashtray and, with an unsteady hand, struck a match and lit the new cigarette. She dragged on it deeply, then blew the smoke into the air, watching it, before she turned again to speak. "No, you wouldn't . . . No drink, no cigarette, no men, I can tell that at a glance." The rudeness stung Carmichael, and the colour mounted to her cheeks.

"All right, all right. I'm sorry, I shouldn't have said that. What good are men anyway? No good at all . . . No good at all. But to get back to our muttons, as my grandmother used to say, I think it was muttons . . ." Carmichael still remained silent. "It's about Charles really. I asked you here about Charles. You see, that day at the mill, I saw you . . . I know you killed him." She stopped and looked at Carmichael to see the effect. There was a slight smile on her heavily lipsticked mouth.

Carmichael's reaction was instant, but controlled. Her body became rigid and her face drained of colour, but she tried to still all other reactions. Her hands remained in her lap, and she did not clasp them tightly or react in any way other than the rigidity and loss of colour.

"Oh yes, I saw you, I was inside the house, and the estate agent man was still in the hall. I was looking out of the window, the side window, you could see the gate from there, and the mill. I saw you. I saw Charles saying something to you—I couldn't hear it, of course, but I could see that he was riled about something. He took a step backwards, didn't he? But he didn't fall . . . You pushed him, you put your hand in the middle of his chest and backwards he went, and disappeared. I couldn't see where he went, but I guessed it was on the wheel, or in the water—it was on

the wheel. If you'd seen him in the morgue afterwards
. . ."

Christine Abbott suddenly took up her glass and emptied
it, got up and went and replenished it at the bar cart, then
came back and stood for a moment, swaying slightly, looking down at Carmichael, who was still silent.

Carmichael had regained something of her composure.
The colour had come back to her face, but her heart was
still racing. Automatically, nurselike, she put her hand to
her chest. She could feel her heart pumping away, a hun-
dred and twenty at least, she thought, and that nurselike
reaction somehow steadied her more. "Oh yes, what are
you going to do about it?" she managed to say, fairly
evenly.

"I could go to the police . . . but I don' wanner do that,
because I'm glad you did it . . . He was a swine, my husband. I hated him, I was glad when he wen' over, over the
top, that's all I saw. I put up a good show with the estate
agent; I screamed, I rushed about; the bloody man couldn't
get his car out. I rushed about calling Charles, Charles, but
I knew where he was. He saw the blood in the water . . . I
was good. I should have been an actress."

Carmichael let Mrs. Abbott ramble on; she was rapidly
becoming more and more composed. Again, she put her
hand up to the artery in her neck, and noted that her pulse
rate was sinking back to normal, about eighty-eight now,
she guessed. She smiled to herself, and Christine Abbott
noticed it and grimaced a little, put the new drink down on
the table and lighted another cigarette. The hand that
lighted it was even more unsteady, and the first match,
before she managed to get the cigarette alight, flew across
the room on to the carpet. Christine Abbott watched it, but
it flickered out.

"Now, a little bargain could be struck between Sister

Carmichael, and Mrs.—Mrs. Charles . . . Mrs. Christine Abbott, couldn't it?"

"How?" asked Carmichael, looking at the woman now sprawled on the settee.

"Well, they're going to have me up, or something. If that kid dies, I could be had up, couldn't I, or something or other?"

"Yes, I suppose you could. I don't know much about these things, but I suppose if Marie died you could be had up for manslaughter."

"Yes, well, I wan' you to do somethin' about it for me. You see, Marie fell down the stairs, right?"

"Wrong, Mrs. Abbott," said Carmichael coldly. Mrs. Abbott went to rise and fell back again.

"It was not 'wrong.' I hit her, I hit her, little bugger, she was yelling and screaming for her Daddy, then she started yelling and screaming at me because I hit her, then she ran out of the room and fell from top to bottom of the stairs, that's how she broke her arm."

"And her leg?"

Christine Abbott shook her head. "No. She ran out of the back door and down the three steps. Crash! Wha' a crash, righ' down those concrete steps, that's when her leg broke. I pulled her up and indoors, in case anyone saw. You can't see much from the other houses, but you can see enough, they're a snoopy lot. I called the ambulance."

"And what do you expect me to do about all this?" asked Carmichael.

"Well, I dunno, but you could put in a good word, you could say that you knew me, and that I wouldn't do such a thing to a child, that you were certain I wouldn't, that you were here at the time—anything."

"How could I be here at the time? I was on duty."

"Well, you're a Sister, you lot stick together, and with you on my side, you could do something, surely. Just speak for me; that bloody Sister Jones, she's against me. You could say . . . you could say . . . I don't know, but somebody in the hospital to help can't be bad; and if you don't, if you don't do something to help me, I shall tell them about Charles, I shall tell them how you pushed him to his death . . ."

Mrs. Abbott, exhausted by this long sentence, closed her eyes, and her head wagged to and fro; then with an effort she opened her eyes wide, picked up the glass with an unsteady hand, and emptied it.

Carmichael's voice was even, steady, because she knew exactly what she was going to do.

"Mrs. Abbott, you may have seen what you say you have seen, but I must tell you there is nothing, nothing at all I can do to help you in the hospital. Little Marie was brought in in a dreadful state, and whatever I said . . . wouldn't help you."

"But you listened. Charles said you listened outside the door when he was talking to Dr. Stephenson. You heard him say she'd got this *fragi* . . . *fragi* . . . *fragilitas,* or whatever it is, something wrong with her bones. You could say you heard that, nobody else seems to know about it. And Charles said you were listening, Charles said . . ."

"I couldn't say that. If she's got that disease she's got it, but she's still been beaten about the head. You haven't got a chance, Mrs. Abbott."

"Then neither have you," answered Mrs. Abbott.

Carmichael did not answer that remark; she was thinking, and again that wonderful feeling was coming over her, a feeling of power, of confidence in her ability to deal with people she didn't want around. Mrs. Abbott was certainly one of those. She waited another few minutes. Mrs. Abbott attempted to get up to get another drink.

Carmichael said, "Let me get it for you." She took the glass over, picked up the whisky bottle, half-filled the glass, put a lump of ice in it, and took it back to Mrs. Abbott. Mrs. Abbott looked at her uncertainly but took the glass from Carmichael's hand. Some of it slopped on to the coffee-table in front of her, so she drank a little, and giggled, and put the glass down. She watched Mrs. Abbott take another swig of the refilled glass. This should knock her out, thought Carmichael, surely.

Within a couple of minutes Mrs. Abbott's head slumped back on to the wide, soft cushion of the settee. Her mouth dropped open, her eyes closed, then she recovered slightly and sat up. "Wha's the matter with me?" she said. "I've had a few, but it's not making any difference to my d-d—" She attempted the word "decision," then gave it up. She picked up the matches, then dropped them again. This time her head did not fall back, but she remained looking vacantly at Carmichael.

Carmichael felt the time was ripe; she rose to her feet. "Will you excuse me a minute, Mrs. Abbott? May I just go to the cloakroom?"

Mrs. Abbott nodded, grinning foolishly. "Do. Do. Do . . . Avail yourself of the fac . . . of the fac . . ."

Carmichael left the room, looked round the hall to assess which was the cloakroom. She opened a door; she was right. There, in the small room, containing lavatory and wash-hand basin, hanging on a row of pegs, was her mac and scarf. She took them down and, carrying them over her arm, draped them on a chair outside the sitting-room door. As she was doing so, a cat ran out of the kitchen, a thin, long tabby, with a white breast and white front paws. It was miaowing piteously, as if for food. It passed Carmichael without a glance and went into the sitting-room, and she heard Mrs. Abbott's voice.

"That bloody cat, that's Marie's bloody cat. Her father got it for her, I don' like it."

Carmichael went back into the sitting-room. The cat was

no longer visible, but Mrs. Abbott was still upright and just draining the glass of whisky that Carmichael had brought her from the bar cart.

"More?" She looked questioningly at Christine Abbott, still standing, and there was no suspicion in the woman's eyes as she looked back at Carmichael.

"Don' min' if I do. Help yourself." She had obviously forgotten that Carmichael had not taken a drink of any kind, and she sat back, her eyes still vacant, while Carmichael replenished the glass again.

Carmichael picked up the cigarette-box, opened it, and offered Mrs. Abbott a cigarette. Mrs. Abbott's fingers shuffled among them, and she dropped two before she managed to hold one in her fingers, stick it in her mouth, and then look round for the matches. Carmichael pushed the box towards her. Mrs. Abbott looked at her. "Trying to get round me . . . be nice to me . . . ? It won't make any difference, won't make any diff . . . difference at all." She struck the match and held it a good inch away from the cigarette; Carmichael saw her chance. The match burned down in Mrs. Abbott's wavering hand, and she dropped it with a muttered "Blast."

Carmichael took the matchbox, lighted a match, and held it to Christine Abbott's cigarette. The woman drew in her breath to get the cigarette going, still with her eyes on Carmichael. Carmichael moved the match slightly sideways and dropped it between the cushions of the settee. It was still alight.

She stood back a little and watched. Mrs. Abbott took another drink and then subsided. She slumped sideways on to the couch, leaning on the end, the cigarette still clamped between her fingers. Carmichael stood and watched, and saw, to her satisfaction, a small curl of smoke come up from between the cushions of the settee. Was that enough? she wondered. She had read about the sponge used to pack these soft cushions and she wondered . . . Would it catch and was it the right type of filling? The smoke-curl grew a little thicker, and she thought of the blood in the stream, and smiled. Mrs. Abbott didn't move. Her eyes closed and she was snoring gently. Carmichael took the cigarette from her fingers and dropped that between the cushions as well . . . You couldn't be too efficient, she thought. Then she walked out of the sitting-room, put on her mac, and tied her scarf round her head. All thought seemed to have stopped, but the feeling of elation was there.

At the front door she felt something touch her leg and looked down. It was the cat.

"Why should you get suffocated? You've done nothing." Carmichael spoke to the cat, surprised at the sound of her own voice. She opened the front door and the animal ran out into the now darkened garden, and Carmichael followed, closing the front door firmly behind her.

Once outside, she tightened the headscarf under her chin, pushing her handbag up under her arm to do so. It was still raining. She walked to the bottom of the drive. There was not a soul in sight. She crossed the road and stood looking at The Laburnums. She could see nothing, no sign of fire, but then the smoke, it was the smoke that killed. Carmichael knew that she had done right; no compassion, she always did it right.

Suddenly something went wrong. The front door of The Laburnums opened and a beam of light shone out into the darkening evening—in the door, swaying, stood Christine Abbott.

Carmichael did not think, did not hesitate. She walked crisply across the road, up the drive, and arrived at the doorway. The eyes of Mrs. Abbott met hers, without understanding, indeed without focusing; she was coughing. Carmichael put her hand in the middle of Mrs. Abbott's chest as she had done with her husband . . . it was a nice feeling. She pushed hard, and although Christine Abbott had one hand holding on to the door frame, it was no good. She was too drunk, too unsteady on her feet. She almost ran backwards, across the hall, and Carmichael saw her crash down, her head just inside the sitting-room door. Carmichael advanced a little further into the hall and smelled a dreadful, pungent smell. She backed out of the front door once more, closed it firmly. That would finish it.

Carmichael waited a little longer at the foot of the drive, concealed by a tall rhododendron bush, but it was quite safe, there was no one about. The front door of The Laburnums did not open again. At last Carmichael started on her walk home. She had just reached the corner of Surbiton Grove when again she felt something brush against her leg. She looked down. It was the cat, the thin, miserable-looking tabby cat, Marie's cat. Carmichael looked down at it; it was already drenched, and it looked up at her and gave the piteous miaow that it had in the house. Carmichael looked round. No one, no one watching. She bent down, picked the cat up, opened her mackintosh, slipped the cat inside, cradling it under her arm. There was no reason in her mind for doing this, no actual feeling of kindness, she just did it. The cat did not struggle, just lay warmly against her, and as Carmichael looked down at its head sticking out from her mac, it began to purr. She walked on, through the rain, towards her own flat, with just one backward glance at Surbiton Grove, where all was now quiet.

She let herself into her flat, put the cat down on the floor, slipped out of her mac, and hung it carefully in the bathroom so that the drips wouldn't go on to the carpet. She spread her headscarf on the side of the bath to dry, methodical as always. Then she looked down at the cat, which was still following her.

Carmichael went through to the kitchen and looked in her store cupboard. What do cats eat? she asked herself almost irritably. What do cats eat? Sardines? Pilchards? She got out a small tin of pilchards, took it to the wall can-opener, and opened it. In the back of her mind were the words, "what a waste," but by the time she had opened the tin, mashed the pilchards up in a small dish, and put it on the floor for the cat and had seen it ravenously attack them, the feeling of waste disappeared. A sudden warm glow went through Carmichael which was completely foreign to her. Not the same elation that followed doing something like she had just done in Surbiton Grove—this was a differ-ent glow. In dealing with Mrs. Abbott there was a feeling of power and omnipotence, as if she were God. But this was something smaller, warmer, comforting. The cat finished the pilchards and licked the dish clean, then looked up at Carmichael with green, round eyes. It walked round the kitchen, smelling the legs of the table and chairs daintily. Carmichael put a saucer of milk down, but the animal was satisfied; it took a couple of laps, again stroked its body against Carmichael, and walked through to the sitting-room.

Carmichael switched on her electric fire. Immediately the cat sat down in front of the one bar that was already throw-ing out a nice warmth and began to wash its face.

Carmichael had never been allowed to have a pet in her whole life. She smiled to herself an unaccustomed, warm smile. "Did you like those? I bet you were hungry. I wonder what they called you?"

The unaccustomed sound of her own voice startled her for a moment, but the cat reacted to it and looked up at her and made a curious little chirping noise. Carmichael sat down. She felt very tired; she must get herself some supper or she wouldn't sleep at all.

The cat came over and jumped on to Carmichael's lap, and went on licking its paws as it lay there in a circle on her knee. She stroked its head absently. It was a strange-looking cat, and as Carmichael stroked it, she felt the bones of its back . . . too thin, she thought. But then Carmichael knew nothing about cats, but she suddenly felt she was going to learn. She was loath to disturb it, but after a time she picked it up bodily and put it in her other armchair. It immediately curled up, put one paw over its eyes, and appeared to go to sleep. Carmichael stood for a moment, looking down at it, then went through to the kitchen to get herself some supper.

On the whole, she thought, a very satisfactory Bank Holiday, and suddenly she was aware that although the cat was making no noise, the flat did not feel the same, and she was no longer aware of the ticking of the clock.

25

On Tuesday morning Carmichael arrived in Out Patients supported by a feeling of euphoria. She felt yesterday had been quite one of the most successful days in her life. Her mind was also preoccupied with the cat. She needed advice, and the first person she met as she came into the department was Mrs. Dixon, the cleaner.

"Good morning, Mrs. Dixon," she said, more affably than usual. Mrs. Dixon turned round, looked at her, realized she had a cigarette in her mouth, which was strictly against the rules, took it out, crushed it underfoot, then picked it up and put it in the bucket. Carmichael pretended not to see it.

This morning was fracture-clinic morning, and the nurses were busy clattering about in the plaster room, getting it ready for the plaster nurse, and the chairs in the waiting-room were being rearranged so that people on crutches and with leg plasters could move about more easily. No matter how carefully it was organized, the fracture clinic appeared chaotic but in actual fact ran pretty smoothly.

Carmichael cast her eyes about the department, then she spoke to Mrs. Dixon again. "Mrs. Dixon, could I have a word with you?" She made her way to her office, conscious of the fact that Mrs. Dixon thought she was going to reprimand her about the cigarette, and as Carmichael sat down at her desk, Mrs. Dixon stood beside her and bridled.

"Do you know anything about cats?" Carmichael looked

at Mrs. Dixon and Mrs. Dixon looked back at her in surprise.

"Cats, Sister? I'll say I do, I've only got seven. Strays, you know, ones I've adopted; then one had kittens, and well . . . they're all doctored now, so no more of that; but, yes, I know about cats."

"Well, I've just got a cat, and wondered if you could give me a bit of advice about . . . they have trays, don't they?"

Mrs. Dixon nodded. "Yes. I put newspaper in mine; I can't afford the cat litter, but it's better to have the litter really."

"Litter?" Carmichael's eyebrows rose and she looked at Mrs. Dixon attentively.

"You want to go out and buy a litter tray, and then a pack of litter, a good, big pack really. If it's only a kitten, still I should get a cat-sized tray, I mean, you'll only have to buy again when it grows."

Carmichael drew a piece of paper towards her; "Cat litter tray," she wrote down, and then underneath, "Cat litter," and underneath that, "Cat food." "Anything else I'll need —besides, of course, tinned cat food. Is that all right?"

Mrs. Dixon nodded. "It's expensive. They love a ping-pong ball, Sister; it's light, you see, and they like chasing it about."

Carmichael wondered about the long, lean tabby she'd brought home from the Abbotts', whether that was at the playing stage. She nodded, but did not add the ping-pong ball to the list. "Thank you, Mrs. Dixon. I'll go and get the things at lunchtime and take them home to my flat and see how the cat's getting on—the kitten, I should say."

"Oh, lovely. Are you going to have it doctored, seen to, you know?"

Carmichael did not reply for a moment, then, "Yes. Is there . . . How do you know if they're male or female?"

Mrs. Dixon explained the procedure and how she would

know if a male cat had been doctored. She obviously thought it highly diverting to be telling all this to a Sister. "I'm so pleased you've got a cat, Sister, you'll love it."

"Why are you pleased?" asked Carmichael curiously. Mrs. Dixon's pleasure was so obviously sincere.

"Well, I mean, a cat, it's a nice thing to have, you won't be lonely, not with a cat."

"I'm not lonely now. I just . . ." Carmichael decided not to continue the conversation, but thanked Mrs. Dixon as she departed with a warm smile. It was obvious that she liked Carmichael better already.

The fracture clinic made the morning pass quickly; the nurses loved it. Three doctors sat in three different clinic rooms, and the patient hobbled in if they had injured their leg or walked in if it was their arm or wrist. If it was their leg, they were taken in in chairs with their leg supported by a board if they had had their plaster removed or just had another cast put on.

Down at the end of the department, a porter with a plaster saw worked hard removing plasters as they came out of the clinic. The whine of the plaster saw made a background noise to the patients' chatter and the clatter of constantly falling crutches.

The appointments office was busy with "See you in a fortnight" or "See you in a week." It was a clinic full of incident, and the patients were jocular and happy, not in most cases particularly ill.

Young men swung in easily through the doors on their crutches, their bodies moving like pendulums in between them. Old ladies came in hesitantly, being helped by ambulance drivers, who handed them over to a nurse, and they were conducted painfully to a seat, where they sat, if they were in plaster, with their leg stuck out in front of them, a constant danger to people passing by.

The nurses flew to and fro; it was like no other clinic, and after it the department had to be cleaned again, so Mrs. Dixon would be back. The porters helped. The plaster all over the floor in the plaster room had to be washed away, and the gullies had to be cleaned so that there was no blocking. It was quick-moving, and usually there were no tragedies.

At last it was finished; the last patient had left and the porters started cleaning. Mrs. Dixon arrived back, giving Sister Carmichael a wide, conspiratorial smile as she walked in. Carmichael did not return it; she'd had enough of that little bit of intercourse, learned what she wanted, and now she was going to slip out, miss her lunch, and get the required cat furniture.

She drove her Mini to the centre of the town, where there was a pet shop. She bought a tray, choosing blue to go with her kitchen. She presumed that was where she'd have to put it. The pack of cat litter was heavier than she had thought, and she got it with difficulty to the car. She bought four tins of cat food, all different types, and decided she'd try them one at a time to see which the cat liked best; then she drove home to her flat.

As she opened the door, the cat came forward and greeted her, its tail erect, making again the strange chirruping noises that Carmichael found pleasant. She put the tray down, and the cat promptly jumped in and inspected it. Carmichael gently shooed it out and put the inch and a half of cat litter in the bottom as the instructions on the bag told her. The cat immediately jumped into the tray again and started to scrape the litter with its front paws. It then sat down and urinated. It was so neat, so automatic that Carmichael was quite amazed at the cat's efficiency.

"Good girl, or boy," she said, and the cat looked up at her as she sat with frowning concentration. Carmichael read the bag. Yes, she must get a spoon; she'd keep it in a jam jar with a little disinfectant, but she'd do all that when she got home this evening.

She stroked the cat as it leapt out of the litter tray, scattering one or two pieces of the white litter round it. Carmichael got a brush, brushed that up, then opened a can of food, put it into a plate, and put it down by the cat. It ate ravenously again, but spilled some of the food round the plate, and Carmichael made a mental note to get her, or him, a proper cat bowl. When the cat had finished the food, she decided to examine its back portion. According to Mrs. Dixon, who Carmichael thought was pretty certain to be right, it was a doctored female. Well, she must think of a name for it. She wouldn't let it out yet . . . now that was another thing she must ask about. She'd heard somewhere that you buttered their feet; she must ask Mrs. Dixon.

The cat rubbed itself round her legs, and she talked to it. "Now I've got to leave you, you've got to be on your own. I'm sorry, but it's better than being in that place where you were, with no food, by the look of it—beastly woman."

She wondered about Mrs. Abbott. Not a word had been said or . . . well, she'd drive by Surbiton Grove and look at The Laburnums on her way back to the hospital. She closed the front door firmly on the cat, which was following her, got into her car, and drove back towards the hospital, with a slight deviation down Surbiton Grove.

The front of the house looked exactly the same as when she'd left it last night. The front door was shut and no windows open. Well, she wondered what the back looked like, but obviously nobody had yet discovered anything, or surely . . . She was glad a full-scale fire hadn't broken out, and just hoped that Mrs. Abbott . . . well, she felt she could rely on the smoke that was already filling that room when she pushed her back in there . . . Surely there couldn't be much doubt. Carmichael's foot went down a little on the accelerator, and she made her way back to the hospital and parked. She looked at her watch; no time for lunch, but she would go up to the rest-room and just have a coffee.

When she got there, Jones was seated in one of the chairs with the television on. She was sipping her coffee and looking moodily at the picture on the screen. "Hallo." She looked up as Carmichael entered. "Didn't see you at lunch. Fracture clinic? Too busy?"

"No, the fracture clinic finished very well. I've reorganized it quite a bit, you know, some of the nurses said it used to go on until two o'clock. I wasn't having that, oh no," said Carmichael firmly. "We finish now in time for lunch. I had to go out to the shops." She decided not to say anything to Jones about the cat.

"Well, I'm bloody fed up," said Jones suddenly, and she looked up at Carmichael, and Carmichael noticed the red, swollen eyes. Jones had been crying.

"What's the matter?" she said automatically and almost without interest, but Jones answered quickly.

"Oh, it was last night. I told you I was going out. I got home a bit late, I was only out with a girl-friend, for God's sake. We took ourselves out to dinner, being Bank Holiday, you know, I thought I'd give her a bit of a treat, it was her birthday, too. I didn't get home till about half past eleven or twenty to twelve. Well, by the time we'd had coffee and talked, and I'd driven her home, and went in and had a natter . . . She works at the Cottage Hospital, and we've got things in common. But when I got home, oh, God . . ."

Carmichael inclined her head questioningly.

"It's Mum, she's a bit senile. You know what they're like, cry at the drop of a hat. The moment I got in the door she started. 'Why are you so late?' 'How could you leave me all this time?' 'I've been by myself getting more and more depressed.' 'It's terrible, you don't think of me at all.' Holy

Mary, I never think of anything else but her, my life's run round her. I don't know how she can say it to me." Jones burst into tears, muttering into her handkerchief, "Sorry, I didn't mean to, but I'm full up, choked, that's all."

"How old is she?" asked Carmichael.

"Eighty-five. Well, she had me last, you see; I was the last of the six, three boys and three girls, all married except me. One's divorced, shouldn't be, we're Catholics, but she damn well is. I've had a chance, a couple, but the last one Mum just queered it, it meant taking her with me, and he didn't want to know. There's promotion too, well, I'd like to be a Nursing Officer, but how can I go to another hospital? How can I move her? She wouldn't move anyway . . . bloody hell." She blew her nose noisily and wiped her eyes.

"Is she bedridden then?"

Jones shook her head and wiped her nose again clumsily. "No, she can get about, but not out, I don't encourage that. I think she'd wander off and forget where she lived. Whenever I go home, I wonder if I'm going to find her there. She did once go out in her night-dress and it was bloody awful." The memory started up more tears.

"Well, I wouldn't like that much myself," said Carmichael.

"I suppose there's always someone, some fool in the family who gets the lot, but if only they'd relieve me, just for a fortnight in the summer. I've asked them, but they're always too busy, or having the house decorated, or one of the children is ill—it's always something, and I'm left. Oh, I did have a fortnight off four years ago, but I don't think I can stand much more of it."

"Why don't you do something about it?" said Carmichael. She put the tips of her fingers together, looking at Jones over the top of them. She had finished her coffee and she glanced at the clock. There were ten more minutes before she was due back on duty.

"Do something about it? Put her in a home, you mean? I couldn't do that, I just couldn't. She'd die, she'd raise hell and even walk out if she wasn't properly supervised. I could pull a few strings, I suppose, but well . . . she is my mother." Jones dried her eyes on the damp, crumpled handkerchief and thrust it into her pocket.

"Well, her life can't mean much to her. Does she read? Does she enjoy television? Is she confused? It sounds as if she is, if she'd walk out like that in her night-dress," said Carmichael.

"No, she doesn't understand the television, she watches the pictures, but she can't read or knit, or do anything like that now. She's got cataracts . . . see?"

"Well, if it were me, and I were you, and I had access to drugs like you have . . . I can't see the point of letting her go on living."

Jones looked at her open-mouthed; it was some seconds before she spoke, then she said, "Carmichael, you really mean that, don't you? You would do that, wouldn't you? But that's euthanasia. I know some people agree with it, but well, we're Roman Catholics, I couldn't do anything like that, even if I could get the drugs, I couldn't."

"Oh, there's ways and means, I'm sure," said Carmichael, her fingertips still together, her eyes, slightly amused, still fixed on Jones. "And if you're a Roman Catholic, you've only got to go to confession and say what you've done and get forgiven. He can't tell, can he? Seal of the confessional, or something." Carmichael's lips turned down in her peculiar smile, and again Jones was silent for some seconds before she stood up as if she couldn't bear Carmichael's company any longer.

"No. It isn't like that, you don't understand Catholicism at all." She looked at the clock. "I've got to go back." She suddenly appeared to have a feeling of revulsion towards Carmichael as she turned away. "I wish you hadn't said that, Carmichael. I wish you hadn't said it as if you really meant it. I mean, would you do a thing like that, if it were your mother?"

Carmichael looked at her steadily. "Of course I would, I'd have no hesitation, I wouldn't let anyone spoil my life like that, and after all, she's getting no joy out of it herself, is she? It would be a kindness."

Jones turned and looked at her as she stood by the door. "I don't think you would when it came to it. I don't think you would. I mean, is your mother still alive?" Carmichael looked at her but did not reply.

"You couldn't do it, of course you couldn't do it," said Jones. She opened the door and went out, leaving it open behind her.

Carmichael got up. Really, the fuss these people made about getting rid of someone. Poor old woman—she was probably miserable, left alone all day; she could quite see why she moaned and groaned when Jones came in late at night. It was reassuring too, to know that Jones had only been out with a girl-friend. For a moment she'd thought . . . Of course not. Jones wasn't attractive. Carmichael smiled again to herself.

Well, she must get back to her Out Patients department. As she walked down the stairs, away from the rest-room, a very comforting thought went through her head. How many times had she heard people say after they'd been offended, crossed, or been done out of something by someone else, "I could kill so-and-so," but how many people did, or could? Not many.

26

Mrs. Danby made her way towards The Laburnums on Wednesday morning. As she walked, the local village clock struck nine, which meant that Mrs. Danby was a little late, but she did not quicken her step; she felt certain that Mrs. Abbott would still be in bed. Since the death of her husband she had rarely got up before midday.

Yesterday had been Mrs. Danby's day at Mrs. James' at Holly Oaks, the job she preferred. She classed Mrs. James as a lady; Mrs. Abbott she did not.

In her right hand Mrs. Danby carried a handbag, in her left, a plastic carrier, containing her apron and the scarf she tied round her head while she dusted. This carrier usually left the Abbotts' house heavier than it went in. Mrs. Danby felt that working at the Abbotts' deserved a few perks, particularly since the death of Major Abbott. While he was alive, if Mrs. Abbott had drunk too much the night before and been sick on the carpet, he would leave a fiver in an envelope for Mrs. Danby, extra to her wages. Or, if he was still there when she arrived, he would apologize and say, "Mrs. Abbott wasn't very well last night, I wonder if you would mind . . ." Mrs. Danby didn't mind, when there was a fiver attached.

How many times had she shampooed bits of the sitting-room carpet where Mrs. Abbott had vomited? Quite a few times. Once, Mrs. Abbott had vomited on the new settee. Then she had had to unzip the Dacron covers from the cushions and wash them, and those and the sponge filling had taken days to dry. Mrs. Abbott had asked her why they had had to be washed, which showed that she must have been pretty drunk when it all happened, for she didn't remember. Now there was no longer Major Abbott. True, since his death there'd been nothing to clear up, but that, she felt, didn't prove that Mrs. Abbott was drinking less, just that perhaps she was able to hold it a little better.

She trudged up the still wet drive. As she did so, she glanced up at the bedroom window, to the left of the door, which was Mrs. Abbott's. It was usually open, but this morning she noticed it was closed. This was rather surprising, because Mrs. Abbott always opened that window before she went to bed, drunk or sober. However, it made little difference.

Mrs. Danby had her own key. As she fumbled for it in her handbag, she thought, Well, a quick look at the bar cart will tell me how much she had last night and the night before. Anyway, she thought, little Marie is out of the way, I won't have her room to do, she's in hospital. Mrs. Danby didn't particularly like children, but neither did she approve of the way Mrs. Abbott hit the child, and she had seen her on one or two occasions knock her clean across the room with a smack across the side of the face. No, Mrs. Danby did not approve, but she felt it was nothing whatever to do with her, and she knew that Major Abbott had been well aware of what happened to the child. Sometimes there had been rows between the two of them about Marie, and Mrs. Abbott's treatment of her.

Mrs. Danby found the key at last and inserted it in the door, thinking as she did so, I'll take a couple of tins of soup when I leave today, I'm short of soup.

She opened the front door and was met by a terrible, pungent smell. Then she saw Mrs. Abbott. She lay half in, half out of the sitting-room. Her legs, one knee flexed, were stretched out on the parquet flooring of the hall, her head and shoulders just inside the sitting-room, her arms flung out at each side of her on the carpet. Mrs. Danby advanced a little and peered into the room beyond. Everything in it seemed black. Mrs. Danby had just time to look at the settee, on which lay the practically disintegrated, burnt cushions, then looked again at Mrs. Abbott's face, congested, the eyes wide open, staring, it seemed at her, before she let out a scream, turned, rushed across the hall, through the front door, down the drive, and along to Holly Oaks. She ran up that drive, rang the bell, and pounded on the door.

It was opened fairly quickly by Mrs. James. "Why, Mrs. Danby, it was your day yesterday." Then Mrs. James got a fuller look at Mrs. Danby's white face.

"What's the matter, come in," she said, and closed the door behind Mrs. Danby, who walked across the hall, which was very similar to The Laburnums', but fully carpeted.

She sat down on the hall chair, gasping, and covered her face with her hands.

"Try and pull yourself together and tell me what's the matter, Mrs. Danby." Mrs. James' voice was severe, yet kind.

"It's Mrs. Abbott, she's dead in there. It's all black, it's horrible, her eyes are wide open. She's dead . . ." Mrs. Danby stumbled over her words, and Mrs. James took her hands firmly away from her face and held them, looking straight at her.

"Now, tell me again—what's happened?"

"It's Mrs. Abbott," said Mrs. Danby, more lucidly, taking her time, now the first awful shock was wearing off. "She's lying there, half in, half out of the sitting-room, and it's all black in there."

"You mean, black, dark, the curtains drawn, you can't see anything?"

"No, no." Mrs. Danby shook her head. "No, the rest of

the room, the furniture, the settee, it's all black, burnt . . ."

"Did Mrs. Abbott smoke?" Mrs. James asked.

"Yes, and drank. I expect she was drunk and dropped a cigarette. They say that sponge stuff . . . I know it's sponge stuff, I had to wash it when she was sick."

Mrs. James shook her head as if she didn't want to hear any more of this. "Well, we'd better walk round. Did you leave the door open?" Mrs. Danby nodded. "Then we'd better go round and make sure she's dead. Come along, pull yourself together, Mrs. Danby." Mrs. James patted Mrs. Danby's shoulder and made her rise, and then both women walked out of the front door and back to The Laburnums and in through the wide-open front door.

Everything Mrs. Danby had said was confirmed as Mrs. James looked at the scene. Horrific. But Mrs. James was a calmer observer than Mrs. Danby. Indeed, Mrs. Abbott was dead. Mrs. James ventured a little further into the sitting-room. The whole room seemed to be blackened—the ceiling, walls, everything—and the smell was atrocious. She looked at what was left of the settee; the cushions and the back seemed to have disintegrated.

"She must, as you said, Mrs. Danby, have dropped a cigarette down by the side of the cushion and set fire to it." She pointed towards the cushions at the side of the settee. Everywhere there was a black dust, over the table, over everything. Mrs. James backed out to where Mrs. Danby was standing, as far away from the body as she could get.

"We'll go back to my house and call the police. Come along, Mrs. Danby. Have you the key?"

Mrs. Danby looked at her dully. "I don't know, I think so."

"Yes." Mrs. James pointed. "It's still in the front door, you must have left it there. Close the door behind you and we'll go back to my house. Bring the key with you." She was efficient and she had taken over, and Mrs. Danby felt reassured. She followed her back to Holly Oaks, and once there Mrs. James rang the police.

"Yes, Surbiton Grove, The Laburnums . . . a fire. Yes, there is someone there, Mrs. Abbott, I think she's dead . . . Yes, I'll ring her doctor." She put the phone down, looked at Mrs. Danby, who was standing beside her, and said: "Go through into the kitchen and make yourself a cup of tea. I'll have one, too."

She turned again to the phone, and after a time Mrs. Danby heard her say, "Dr. O'Rorke, the police advised me to ring you, it's Mrs. Abbott . . . I'm afraid she's dead . . . Yes, I have seen your car there and I imagined you were the family doctor . . . Yes, a fire. Thank you." She put the phone down and sat there, obviously wondering if there was anyone else she should ring. She went through into the kitchen and joined Mrs. Danby, who was standing, still trembling, waiting for the kettle to boil.

"Has she any relatives, do you know?"

"Yes," Mrs. Danby nodded. "She's got a sister in Derby. She came once, but they didn't get on awfully well. I think that's all she's got. The sister is married and lives in Derby, but I don't know her address."

"Well, somebody will have to get in touch with her, probably we could leave it to the police. And then there's Marie. She's in hospital, though, isn't she? We can leave that for the moment to Dr. O'Rorke; he must inform the sister and the child."

Mrs. Danby made the tea, poured it out, and sipped it thankfully. "Oh, I'm so glad you were in, Mrs. James, thank you so much. I don't know what I'd have done if you'd been out, and if you hadn't lived so near."

Mrs. James also sipped her tea and nodded. "Have you got some sugar in that? You're shocked and it's good for shock," she said to Mrs. Danby, and Mrs. Danby nodded.

"She drank, she drank such a lot, you see. I mean, I had to clean up after her and Major Abbott . . . well . . . that's why little Marie . . ."

"Mrs. Danby, do you mind?" Mrs. James broke in hastily but firmly. "I would rather not get involved in this, if you don't mind. Of course, I was quite willing to help you over this disastrous time this morning, but I don't wish to know any of the details, do you understand?"

Mrs. Danby nodded miserably, because she would have liked to have told Mrs. James a great deal more. They finished their tea, and Mrs. Danby automatically washed up the cups and saucers and emptied the teapot. At that moment they heard the police car as it drew up outside The Laburnums.

"You'd better go back now, and take your key," said Mrs. James. "You can tell them that you told me and that it was I who rang them and I've rung her doctor."

"Aren't you coming with me, Mrs. James?"

Mrs. James shook her head. "No, I don't think that is necessary—if they want me they can call here." She was firm.

Mrs. Danby nodded and reluctantly made her way again down the drive of Holly Oaks and along the road to The Laburnums, where two policemen stood by the front door. Mrs. James watched them from her kitchen window, where she could see through the shrubs. She watched Mrs. Danby speak to the policemen and the policemen nod, and saw Mrs. Danby insert the key in the lock of The Laburnums' front door and disappear inside. Another policeman got out of the panda car and followed them. At that moment Mrs. James heard a wailing sound; it was the ambulance. She stood there, transfixed, for some time. Another police car, another man, this time in plain clothes, got out, carrying a box. Camera? Mrs. James wondered. She stayed watching, then a car drew up and Dr. O'Rorke, whom Mrs.

James knew because he was her doctor as well, got out and walked into the house.

Ten minutes or so later, a stretcher was taken from the ambulance into the house, and then it emerged loaded with the body of Christine Abbott covered with a blanket. Mrs. James shivered slightly. There would be a lot to tell her husband this evening. She turned away from the window; she had seen enough. The Abbotts had never been particularly desirable neighbours—he had been a bumptious little man, and Mrs. Abbott . . . well, almost everyone who lived in Surbiton Grove knew that she drank. Then there was little Marie. Mrs. James pushed aside the thought of the child. Anyway, when it had all blown over, she hoped that whoever took the house would be a better type of neighbour, and she hoped they would play bridge. The Abbotts had not played bridge.

Suddenly, she realized that the police or Dr. O'Rorke, or someone, might come round to her house to question her, and she went across the hall, picked up her handbag, refurbished her lipstick, and patted her hair into place. Well, if they came, she was ready for them.

27

Wednesday morning was a quiet morning in Out Patients; only three clinics, and none of these needing a lot of nursing supervision, such as dressings, or bandaging, or injections, so the atmosphere was relaxed.

As Carmichael entered the department, Mrs. Dixon made straight for her. "How's the little kitty then, Sister?" she asked.

With seven cats of her own, Carmichael took this to be a genuine interest, so answered very fully and less coldly than usual. "Oh, very well, I think. I got the litter tray as you suggested, and the litter, and she used it at once; clever, aren't they?"

"Oh yes, they know at once, and they're clean, too, they're sweet little things," said Mrs. Dixon.

"I'm worried about letting her out still, I don't want her to run away."

"Oh no. If she's very little, you'll have to keep her in for quite a while. If she isn't . . . How old is she?"

"I'm not quite sure, she's not a tiny kitten, about half-way grown up, I should think. A tabby cat." Carmichael prevaricated purposely.

"Well, if she's not quite a kitten, just a young cat, I should keep her in for a week after you've buttered her paws. I know they say it's an old wives' tale, but . . ." She smiled widely.

"I see. Well, thank you. I'll do that, whether it's an old wives' tale or not. She seems to have settled down. She likes me to put the electric fire on, and she ate a whole tin of the food when I got home last night." Carmichael was unusually wordy and Mrs. Dixon noted it. It'll make her more human, having an animal about the place, she thought to herself, it'll make her different.

She nodded vigorously. "She may need a bit more than a small tin a day, Sister; she may, as she gets older, need a big tin, and some fish sometimes they like, and chicken." She nodded wisely.

But Carmichael thought the conversation had gone on long enough and the nurses would be remarking on it, so she dismissed Mrs. Dixon with a "Well, thank you very much, Mrs. Dixon, for your help, I'll remember all that," and she pointedly shuffled some notes together on her desk and opened one set of them. Mrs. Dixon took the hint and disappeared. Carmichael was left thinking about the cat. She'd keep it in a good week. She didn't want it wandering back to Surbiton Grove and The Laburnums; not that there was anyone there now, but after all, someone might recognize it. That worried her a little, but she decided that the treatment it had had there probably wouldn't encourage it to go back, and the treatment it was going to have with her would encourage it to stay.

Carmichael had so enjoyed yesterday evening with the cat. The moment she had had her supper and sat down in front of the television, and, of course, fed the cat, it had jumped on to her knees and curled up purring, and she had sat watching the programme with a curious sense of companionship, and not a sign of that horrible feeling of loneliness, and someone beside her, watching her.

She'd done a little more to organize the cat, too. She had taken home with her, from the hospital stores, a large cardboard box, in which she'd put the tray with its litter. It was easy to clean; she had got a special spoon and stood it in a jar of disinfectant, and now the cardboard box prevented the cat from splattering litter all over the floor when it jumped out. It seemed not to mind the cardboard box at all, indeed it had rubbed its nose round the corners and smelled it all round.

Carmichael found the cat's actions diverting and companionable; yes, she had enjoyed the evening with it; in fact, the flat seemed quite different with the cat there. There was another woman in the flats who had a dog, so Carmichael imagined there would be no difficulty about keeping the cat, and it would soon, after a week or so, go downstairs and out of the back door if it wished. The back door into the small garden was usually open. Yes, Carmichael was very pleased with the new arrangement and her new companion.

The morning progressed easily, as Carmichael had known it would. The nurses came to her one by one, asking to go to lunch, and she nodded, and then followed them.

Sister Jones brought her tray to Carmichael's table but was rather silent, and looked once or twice furtively at Carmichael, much to the latter's amusement. How stupid they are, Carmichael thought. Here's this woman, burdened down with this stupid old mother, and she won't do anything about it, because, I suppose, she's frightened. Her religion holds her in check. She smiled to herself as she ate her roast beef and Yorkshire pudding.

"How's the children's ward, Sister Jones?" she asked, and there was a sarcastic note in her voice, which Jones must have missed, for she answered readily enough.

"Oh, all right. We're full now, change for us. Little Marie Abbott's better. Her mother's not been in this morning though—not that the child's asked for her. She seems happier, and she's managing to eat more. She has to be fed, of course, her two arms are . . . The one that had the drip in is still sore, and of course the other one is still in plaster. But when you feed her, she seems to enjoy it, especially the minced chicken. But then most children do; minced chicken is one of their favourites."

"Oh, really." Carmichael listened to this piece of information without interest, but she was glad to hear that Mrs. Abbott had not turned up. It must mean that she, Carmichael, had done her job well on Monday evening. She wondered how soon Mrs. Abbott would be found; she was surprised that the hospital hadn't been notified by now. But, of course, Mrs. Danby might not go in before this morning. She wondered what Mrs. Abbott and the house would look like. She had seen, on television, rooms that had been smoked out with this foam, and they'd not been a pretty sight. She smiled, a little more broadly, as she pushed aside a rather tough piece of beef, and Jones noticed it.

"Not very good is it, or the Yorkshire pudding? They shouldn't attempt Yorkshire pudding, they make 'em about ten in the morning, and then put 'em in the oven, that's why they're like this." Carmichael nodded. She was not interested in the Yorkshire pudding.

Both Sisters went up to the rest-room for coffee, but little was said, and Jones thumbed through the *Radio Times*, obviously not wanting to open again yesterday's discussion. This amused Carmichael, and she merely remarked, as she got up to go back to her department, "How's your mother then, better today?"

"Yes, thank you, she's all right, she's much better today, I was in last night, you see." Jones answered quickly, and Carmichael nodded.

"That's all right then," she said. "As long as you stay in, that's all right." She gave Jones a sideways look and went out of the rest-room and back to her department.

The afternoon was fairly quiet, too, only Dr. Stephenson taking the paediatric clinic, which would need two nurses; and minor ops in the Out Patients theatre. Carmichael sat

down at her desk and looked at the list which Staff Nurse
Baker had placed there, the list of minor operations to take
place there this afternoon.

No. 1. Removal of wart from neck—Angela Bean, age 22
No. 2. Removal of lipoma from top of head—Mr. Rippon,
age 67
No. 3. Removal of wart from eyelid—Mrs. Agatha Jones,
age 82
No. 4. Removal of loose fingernail—Mrs. Webster, age 40
No. 5. Removal of wart from side of mouth—Mrs. Sey-
mour, age 52

All the operations were to be done under a local anaesthetic, so two nurses could cope with them easily.

She could hear a clatter from the operating theatre as the
nurses laid up trolleys, and made her way down to inspect
that they were properly done.

At half past two, the waiting-room began to fill with children and mothers, and, in a few cases, a child with both
father and mother. She could tell the ones for minor ops at
a glance; their apprehension showed.

Sister Carmichael remembered that she had something
else to check and went along to the theatre and spoke to the
theatre nurse. "There are one or two warts; they'll need
sectioning, nurse. Have you got section jars?"

The nurse looked round the theatre hastily. "No, Sister,
I've forgotten them, sorry, I'll get them straight away," she
said, and Carmichael nodded, turned away, and went back
to her office. It was that kind of thing that made a good
Sister, she thought complacently. It was good for the
nurses to know that she had her eyes on everything.

28

Sister Jones came down from the rest-room a little later than the others. She had gone to lunch late, so put her feet up for ten minutes after they had gone, then she came downstairs and started along the corridor towards the children's ward.

On her way, she met the mortuary porters, wheeling between them the mortuary trolley, with its domed top, covered with a purple cloth with a cross on it, the piece of reverence the hospital gave to the dead. Sister Jones stood back against the wall, and as it passed, she crossed herself; but the porters drew up suddenly, the one in front stopping the one at the back in his tracks.

"Bet you don't know who's under there?" said the porter.

Jones looked slightly scandalized and then rather fearful. "It's not one of the staff, is it?"

The porter shook his head. "No, but you knew her nevertheless, you'll be surprised when I tell you," he said. He was an elderly man with grey hair and a cigarette-kippered upper lip.

"Well, who is it then?" said Jones rather irritably. She hated this dallying in the corridor with a corpse, but the porter closed one eye slowly and said, "Want to guess?"

Jones shook her head and made as if to go on, and the porter was afraid he'd lose the climax to his surprise. "It's Mrs. Abbott, that little girl's mother, the one on the ward, the one that got bashed up, you know, that's who's under there.''

"It isn't!" Jones' eyes rounded, and the porter was satisfied by the amount of surprise on her face.

"Oh yes, it is," he said. "Got drunk, caught herself alight, smoked herself out. Nice mess, I believe. The ambulance chap said it was 'orrible, it was like a, well . . . a black cell, he said.''

"No! First her father, and now her mother, it hardly seems possible," said Jones, gazing at the trolley in disbelief.

"Well, it's possible, all right, somebody called the police to the house this morning. I think it was the cleaner lady. She's been dead about thirty hours, the medic said, so there you are. Must have been Bank Holiday, and she celebrated it by getting herself stoned, and then dropped a cigarette or a match, or something, and there you are. Nice way to end up." Having broken his surprise and seen the reaction, he started pulling the trolley again and said to the porter at the back, "Come on, let's get her tidied up then.''

"Tidied up?" queried Jones.

"Yes, they've got her sister coming to see her, don't know where she comes from, the Midlands, I think. She's going to be here in half an hour, so we're going to put the body straight in the Chapel of Rest, arrange it a bit, to look a bit better, you know. Be a bit of a shock to the sister, I expect.''

The two porters trundled the trolley down the corridor, and the one in front held open the big green door which led on to the yard, across which lay the mortuary. The trolley was pushed through the doors, the front one holding them open and then letting them bang behind him, until the trolley was hidden from view. Only the noise its wheels made as it clattered across the yard outside could be heard.

Jones stood for a moment looking at the green door through which the trolley had vanished. She could hardly believe it. Father and mother both gone, little Marie was an orphan now. She wondered fleetingly about the sister, whether she would take her, then dismissed it from her mind; the child at the moment was not fit to go anywhere and wouldn't be for weeks. Dr. Stephenson—she must tell him. He was in Out Patients. She glanced at her watch—twenty to three. He'd be there by now. She turned on her heel and went back along the corridor and out into the covered way that led to Out Patients.

Arrived there, she went in to Carmichael and said, "I'd like a word with Dr. Stephenson, if you don't mind, Sister Carmichael. May I use your phone?"

"Certainly," said Carmichael, pushing the phone towards her.

Sister Jones picked up the receiver and dialled the children's ward. "I'm over in Out Patients, Staff Nurse, I'll only be about ten minutes, I have to see Dr. Stephenson. Everything all right over there?" She nodded, and put the phone down, then with a brief "Thanks" to Carmichael, she went towards Dr. Stephenson's clinic, but Carmichael called softly after her. "I think he's got a patient in there at the moment—at least, he's seeing the mother. Can you wait a minute?" She knows, thought Carmichael, someone has told her. She knows that Mrs. Abbott is dead; a thrill of excitement ran through her which didn't show on her impassive face.

Sister Jones came back to Carmichael's office. "May I sit down?" she said.

Carmichael motioned to the only other chair in her office. "Do. Anything the matter?" she asked innocently.

Jones gave her a long stare and then decided to tell her. "I've just met the mortuary porters taking a body to the morgue, to the Chapel of Rest. Actually it was Mrs. Abbott, Marie's mother. She's dead."

Carmichael hardly stirred in her chair, but she did turn a

little more towards where Jones was sitting. "Really," she said. "How did that happen then?" Her face showed amusement rather than anything else, but Jones, composing hastily in her mind what she was going to say to Dr. Stephenson, hardly noticed it.

"Yes, burned or choked to death with smoke or something. That's what the porter said. 'Stoned out of her mind' was the expression he used, but I don't know how he learned that—you know what these porters are."

"Yes, I do," said Carmichael. "They're usually the ones who get at the truth. They talk to the ambulance men, talk to anybody."

Jones nodded. "That's right," she said. "They're usually the ones who get to know everything first. Ah, do you think I can go in now?" A patient's mother came out of Dr. Stephenson's clinic, and Carmichael rose, anxious to show Jones that she was mistress of the situation. She made her way towards Dr. Stephenson's clinic room, saying over her shoulder to Jones as she did so, "I'll see."

Carmichael came out almost immediately and said to Sister Jones, "Yes, he says to go in." Jones walked into Dr. Stephenson's clinic and closed the door behind her.

Carmichael went back to her office and sat down in her chair, pushing her hands against her desk and tipping the chair slightly back. She looked up at the ceiling and her lips pursed together. The tip of her tongue ran quickly round them. She put her hand up to the back of her head and felt the straggly bun. I must get my hair cut tomorrow. I'll ask Winter who is the best hairdresser to go to. She'll know, she thought. She was conscious of an immense feeling of relief. After all, she had pushed Mrs. Abbott pretty firmly back into that smoke-filled room, but you never knew. Well, it is nice to know when one has been thoroughly successful.

Jones came out of Dr. Stephenson's room after about ten

minutes, and the nurse in charge of the clinic called the next mother and child in.

Jones poked her head round Carmichael's office. "He says we'll have to tell little Marie, but there's no rush. Poor little soul."

Carmichael could see she was really upset. "Poor little soul," she said, "lucky little soul, I'd say, being rid of a pair like that."

"I wonder what the sister is like, maybe she'll . . ." said Jones reflectively.

"I don't expect she'll want her either. Have to go into care, I expect." Carmichael's voice was calm and detached, and Jones thought, How callous she is, and at that moment disliked Carmichael intensely.

"Well, I must get back to the ward," said Jones abruptly. Carmichael nodded and Jones disappeared.

In the Out Patients department, after about an hour had passed, Carmichael suddenly had the urge to see Mrs. Abbott. She got to her feet and called one of the nurses. "Nurse, I'm just going over to the hospital for a moment. Is everything all right?"

The nurse nodded. "Yes, Sister, everything's all right, we're well up to time. Dr. Godfrey has only another couple of patients to see, and they're old ones."

Carmichael nodded. "Right then, I won't be a moment." She walked with her rapid step out of the department and over into the hospital.

When she arrived at the big, wide green door that led across the yard to the mortuary, she glanced to left and right to see if anyone was watching her. Not that it particularly mattered, but . . . no, a white-coated doctor passed the end of the passage going towards the front hall but didn't even look in her direction, and a nurse pushed open the Casualty doors to her right and disappeared, again without looking at her.

Carmichael pulled the big green door towards her, slipped round it into the yard; no one there, no porters, no delivery vans, nothing. She walked across the yard and turned the handle of the mortuary door. Sometimes they locked it, but not always . . . it was open. The cold struck her as she went in, and she shivered slightly, then turned to her right, into the Chapel of Rest.

The chapel smelled of cold and damp, but there was no one there. Carmichael had wondered if the sister might have arrived, but no, there was no one. In the middle, on a slablike table, lay Mrs. Abbott, all ready for the visit of her sister. Carmichael drew near and looked down at the dead face. It looked slightly congested and livid, and the nose and chin more pointed in death than they had appeared to be in life. Some attempt had been made to make the fair hair look natural; it had been brushed back from the forehead, and a curl pulled round on to the temple. Carmichael looked more closely and noticed that the hair was full of a black powder—the burnt foam, yes, that's what did that. She wondered what the smart room looked like now and smiled to herself. The sheet was drawn right up to Mrs. Abbott's chin, and Carmichael did not attempt to touch the body. She looked up at the small, altarlike edifice at the back of the room, two brass candlesticks and two vases of dahlias. They looked ugly and vulgar in this cell-like room. Just what Christine Abbott deserved, Carmichael thought, looking down again at the dead face with contempt. She turned away, walked out of the Chapel of Rest and back to her own department.

The same impulse that had made Carmichael go to the Chapel of Rest to see Christine Abbott impelled her later to go to the children's ward. "Is Sister on?" she asked one of the nurses, slipping by, and the nurse nodded. "Yes, Sister Carmichael, she's in her office. Shall I . . . ?"

Carmichael shook her head and walked into the ward.

"May I come in, Sister Jones?" she asked formally, and Jones nodded and got up. Her attitude towards Carmichael since the conversation she had had with her about her mother had, much to Carmichael's amusement, subtly changed. It was as if she were regarding Carmichael with new eyes. This did not displease Carmichael.

"I just wondered if I could have a look at little Marie? I saw her come into Casualty, you know." Sister Jones looked surprised. Carmichael had shown little, or no, interest in the child's condition and had hardly listened when Jones had told her about it. True, she had asked once or twice about Marie, but Jones felt it had been done merely to make conversation rather than out of interest, or compassion for the child.

"Why, yes, of course. She really is much better, you'll see an improvement since you saw the poor kid come into Casualty that day."

"I'm sure, with your tender, loving care." Carmichael smiled her slightly downward smile, and Jones looked sharply at her, suspecting sarcasm, but Carmichael seemed genuine enough in spite of the smile.

Marie's bed was situated near Sister's office so that she could keep an eye on her. One arm was still encased in plaster, from the small hand to the elbow. The child was half sitting up, leaning back on the pillows behind her. She looked up as the two women approached. The eye which had been closed when Carmichael had seen the child come through Casualty, closed and distorted with the blow it had received, was now open, though surrounded by black and yellow bruising. She smiled at Sister Jones.

"Hallo, Marie. Here's another Sister come to see you." The one blue eye regarded Carmichael. The other eye, with the sutured lid, was still covered, but the child managed to smile, a small, timid smile.

"Miss Grant, the social worker," said Jones, aside to Carmichael, "bought her this Teddy. Isn't he beautiful?" The child's eyes turned to it. It was a white fluffy bear, small and easy to handle, and Marie's good arm, though still bandaged at the elbow where the drip needle had been, encircled it, the small hand rubbing its tummy affectionately, and her smile became a little broader.

"Is Mummy coming?" Marie asked, and looked straight at Jones. Jones shook her head and the child's eyes turned to Carmichael.

"Not today, she's rather busy, not today," said Jones hastily, and added, "Would you like a drink of orange, or anything?" The child shook her head.

"Well, goodbye," said Carmichael abruptly. The child looked up at her but did not answer, and Jones and Carmichael walked away from the bed.

"How's her leg?" asked Carmichael. "She certainly looks better about the face, and I suppose the greenstick fracture of the wrist is not too bad. But the leg, I heard it was compound?"

"Yes, not often a kid gets a compound fracture like that, goodness knows how it happened."

"A lot happened in that house that we shall never know about," said Carmichael. "Thank God she's rid of them both, neither of them can hurt her again, that's something."

"Yes, but it's her mother and father, after all. You see how she asked for her mother, even after all that. The maternal tie is very great, you know." She said it with what Carmichael took to be underlying meaning. The maternal tie! Poor Jones to that batty old mother, and that poor kid to her sadistic, drunken parent!

Carmichael thought that Sister Jones and a great many other people were mad in their attitude to this paternal and maternal tie, but she said, "Well, personally I am only too grateful that the child is not at risk any more, at least from her parents, very grateful."

"Yes, I suppose it's fate, him being killed, and then the mother. God works in a mysterious way His wonders to perform," said Jones, looking piously, and at the same time rather pointedly, at Carmichael.

"He does indeed," said Carmichael, and this time her smile was really broad, not downwards, but the corner of her lips went up in a real smile, which Sister Jones could not understand.

"Well, thanks for letting me see her. I wanted to know how she was getting on, and I'm glad nothing more can happen to her. As you say, God moves . . ." On this Carmichael left the ward. As she did so, she longed more than ever to say to Jones, or to somebody, "In this case it wasn't God, or Fate, or Accident, it was Carmichael working her wonders."

As she walked away from the children's ward, she suddenly realized that her hay fever had disappeared. When? She tried to recollect, but there had been so much . . . Was it after . . . She glanced down at the floor as she walked along. Was it after the first . . . or the second . . . Try as she would, she couldn't remember. The tissues in her drawer in Out Patients had remained unused since . . . Millstream House . . . or was it Monday . . . The Laburnums? She couldn't remember, but it was pleasant to be able to breathe freely through her nose.

29

A few evenings later Carmichael was driving home, and, as usual at this hour, she got caught in a small traffic jam, in a bottle-neck in the middle of town. It was always the same; there were traffic-lights dividing the four-road junction, but as often as not, if there were six or seven cars in front of her, it would turn red again as soon as you got there. Usually this didn't irritate Carmichael, but this evening she was rather anxious to get home to . . . she hadn't named the cat yet, but she was anxious to get home to it.

She sat waiting for the traffic to move again, and when the lights changed, all the cars crawled forward. Carmichael reached the traffic-lights, and just as she had anticipated, they turned red, and she sat there again, waiting.

She turned her head to the left and saw something she had probably noticed on her way home before, but this evening it seemed to have more significance. It was a church, bounded by railings, and a large notice-board proclaimed it to be Our Lady of Lourdes. A Roman Catholic church. She idly looked at the board, "Times of Masses," and then at the bottom in the same gold lettering, she noticed, "Confessions 6–7 P.M." Carmichael's heart beat a little faster. She thought of her conversation with Jones. Well, if you wanted to tell someone, here was your chance; she glanced at her watch. It was five minutes to six. "God works in a mysterious way." She thought again of Jones, the seal of the confessional; rather fun.

The lights changed. Instead of proceeding straight forward towards her flat, she turned left and continued a little way up the road, past the church, to where the double yellow lines ended, and parked her car. She got out, locked it, and stood turning the keys round and round. She'd left her handbag inside, but that didn't matter; she was certainly not going to put any money in the offertory box or whatever they called it in this particular church.

Carmichael walked back and round to the front gate, read the notice again. Yes . . . "Confessions 6–7 P.M." She walked up the path and into the open church door, through the small porch, pushed open the inner door, and then was in the church itself. She closed the door softly behind her. She was rather surprised that there were so few people, but perhaps nobody had anything to confess. There were two women kneeling near the altar, but in different pews, and one woman opposite what Carmichael realized was the confessional. She slid in behind this woman and, out of habit, knelt down. But her mind was not yet on what she was going to say; she was too busy taking in her surroundings.

The church certainly had a nice feeling, but Carmichael did not agree with graven images. She knew little or nothing about Catholicism, except what had been taught her during training days, when they had to know about various patients' beliefs. She recognized the statue of St. Anthony, and, of course, pride of place was given to Our Lady of Lourdes. Carmichael thought it garish and overcoloured. There was a circle of stars at the back of the head, a pious look on the face, and the hands joined together in supplication. Carmichael gazed at it for some time, then began to compose what she was going to say.

The woman in front of her got up, and Carmichael whispered to her as she did so, "Am I next, after you, I mean?"

The woman nodded. "Yes, there aren't many here tonight, not yet anyway, maybe later." Carmichael inclined her head to the two women up in the front.

"They've been in; he was early tonight, they're only saying their penances . . ." The woman looked at Carmichael rather curiously, but Carmichael withdrew her eyes from her. What she really wanted was to watch which door the woman went in; she didn't want to go in and fall over the priest. There were two doors, and the woman opened the right-hand one. It closed behind her, and Carmichael listened to see if she could hear anything being said. No . . . the doors cut off all communication.

At that moment one of the women at the front got up and walked out of the church, banging the door noisily behind her, and Carmichael frowned. Then she got up off her knees and sat in the pew and waited.

About ten minutes, or less, went by. The woman came out of the confessional, leaving the door ajar, and nodded to Carmichael. She then went forward to the front of the church, slipped into a pew, felt in her pocket and got out a rosary, and started to run it through her thumb and finger.

Her penance. And now, I suppose, she's forgiven everything, Carmichael whispered to herself contemptuously. Then she got up, and for a moment a feeling of nervousness came over her, then she dismissed it. What had she to fear? Nothing. It was just that the situation was unusual to her; she'd never been in a Catholic church before, let alone a confessional, but it would be such joy, such a joy to tell; she couldn't resist it.

She slid out of the pew, walked along the tiled floor, round the back of the font, down to the confessional. At the door, she hesitated, just for a second, then squared her shoulders, went in, closed the door firmly behind her, and found herself in almost utter darkness. The only light filtered through the grille, behind which she could see the vague outline of the priest's white face.

Her feet encountered the hassock, and she pulled it out and knelt down. She found there was a small shelf on which she could put her arms, but she said nothing.

The priest murmured something which ended, "How long since your last confession?"

"I've never been to confession before, I'm not a Catholic. Am I allowed in here?" Carmichael's voice was brisk. She wanted to know, so she asked, and although the situation was slightly intimidating, it was also, to Carmichael, slightly ludicrous. She saw the priest stir, and saw his clasped hands raised up to his chin, as if he was resting his hands on them as he said, "I see, my child. Have you a wish to join us, to become a Roman Catholic? Is that what you have come to tell me?"

"No, not at all. I've come to confess something to you. Is that allowed, as I'm not a Catholic?"

"Well, of course, my child, I'm here to help anyone. What is it you want to tell me?"

Carmichael paused. The sense of drama in this small, enclosed place was strong, and she was enjoying it, talking to a man who couldn't see her, a complacent man, who spent so much of his time listening to the small misdemeanours of his flock, and she wished she could see his face more plainly when she spoke. She peered through the grille more closely, but could see little more than the outline. However, his voice would give him away.

Her momentary silence encouraged the priest to say more. "Come, come, my child, don't be afraid, anything you tell me is in the strictest confidence. You can tell me anything you wish. Don't hesitate to unburden yourself, to tell it to me is to tell it to God himself. If you're not a Catholic, perhaps you don't understand that, but that is how it is."

He stopped speaking, and Carmichael felt encouraged by his wish to hear what she had to say. She wondered if he didn't get sick and tired of hearing tales of adultery, tales of stealing, or small lies, swear-words, a sex problem. Well, she had nothing to tell him that would bore him, so she began. "Well, Father," she said, "I've killed two people and I thought I would like to tell someone about it."

There was a moment's silence, and Carmichael could see that the priest had withdrawn his hands from his face and was sitting a little straighter. She smiled.

"Killed two people, my child? That is a very grave sin. Are you sure . . . ?"

"Am I sure I want to tell you, or am I sure I killed them?"

"Both, my daughter," said the priest, and his voice was a little more animated, but doubting.

"Well, the first one, I pushed into the river, and he fell on a water-wheel and was crushed to death." Carmichael waited, and the priest waited, then it was he who spoke again. "Now, my child, are you quite sure of this? That was a local death, was it not? I read about it in the paper, and he fell accidentally."

"No. He didn't fall accidentally, I pushed him. I wanted him dead, you see, and I pushed him. It was better that he was dead; he was not a good man."

"It is not for us to judge whether a man is good or bad, it is for God alone . . . 'Vengeance is mine,'" said the priest, but his voice did not show that he was impressed by what Carmichael had said. He didn't believe her.

The record in the paper was obviously the truth to him, so Carmichael continued. "Then his wife, she's dead, too. I set fire to her furniture and she died. She died too." Carmichael waited. This time there was a longer silence.

"Now, my daughter," said the priest, and there was none of the urgency, none of the amazement in his voice that Carmichael had so expected. "My child, was this lady . . . was she also a wicked person?"

"Oh, very, a very wicked person indeed. She bashed her child about, a little girl."

"And the man . . . how was he wicked?" asked the priest.

Carmichael began to realize that he was talking as if to one slightly demented, and this made her angry. "He bashed my Mini, my new car, and broke the headlamp, and didn't even stop to see what he'd done."

"He ran into your Mini . . ."

Carmichael corrected him. "He backed into it," she said.

"He backed into your Mini, and so you killed him. Was that the reason?"

"No, there were other things . . . But I think the Mini, the fact that he did that to my new Mini, that made me kill him, more than anything else he'd done," said Carmichael. The priest, she could see, had turned away again, and she saw him in profile through the grille.

"I see, I see. But I hardly know what to say to you in view of all this, my child. Of course, you're not a Roman Catholic, and I can't give you absolution . . ."

"Absolution!" Carmichael laughed. "I haven't come to you for absolution, I've come because I want to tell someone, that's all."

"I was going to say I couldn't give you absolution because you're not a Roman Catholic, but if there is anything else I can do to relieve this . . . this great weight there must be on your conscience, or you feel to be on your conscience . . ." It was obvious that the priest found himself to be at a loss.

"No, there's nothing at all you can do. I just wanted to tell you, that's all. Both people are now dead and there's nothing whatever you can do about it. But I felt the need to tell someone, and after all, the confessional is the right place, isn't it?"

Carmichael could see the priest's face. This time his

hands were locked again under his chin and he was vigorously rubbing his chin with his thumb. She half-rose from the hassock she was kneeling on, but his voice stopped her.

"Have you . . . have you told anyone else all this? I mean, your doctor?" the priest asked, and there was a sound of helplessness in his voice that really amused Carmichael.

"Oh-h, you're thinking I'm making it up, and that I should go and see my doctor and make an appointment to see a psychiatrist, is that it, Father?" she said, and her voice was light.

"Well, as you can imagine, one hears a great many things when one is listening to confessions. Sometimes people feel the need to make up things, so that they can be forgiven, to dramatize themselves, to make themselves slightly more important, and I wondered perhaps . . ."

"No, not that. Not that at all," said Carmichael. "I have told you the truth. I killed two people, three actually, two women and a man. It's nice to have told you, because I'm very pleased I've done it. And when one has achieved something, it's nice to tell, don't you agree?"

"Yes, I suppose I do agree, yes, I do agree . . . But you mustn't feel . . . Do you live alone? Perhaps you're lonely. We do have church social meetings, and we would be delighted to welcome you."

"No, I don't think I need to join a club, as they put it in women's magazines, Father," said Carmichael, and again her voice was light and jocular. "You've been very kind to listen and that's all I wanted, I'll leave you now." The priest automatically raised his hand as if to bless her, and then the hand dropped out of sight.

Carmichael was well satisfied. She felt, as the priest had said, as if a great burden had been lifted from her, not because she had confessed, but because at least one other human being knew just what Carmichael could do—that is, of course, if he believed her . . . And somehow or other it didn't matter a lot if he did or not.

She got up from the hassock, opened the door of the confessional and closed it behind her, went into the light of the church, and walked quickly out. She felt much better. Not that she'd felt bad before, but not only had she told another human being, but she had shocked that human being. He didn't believe her; probably no one would, but she had shocked him, and that was pleasant. After all, when she told before, way back in St. Jude's, they hadn't believed her. People needed jerking out of their complacency . . . look at Jones.

Carmichael turned into the street and walked up to her car. A slight drizzling rain had started, and she walked with lowered head. Suddenly she felt herself embraced by a pair of strong arms. She stopped and the arms dropped away from her.

"I'm so sorry," a warm voice said, and Carmichael looked up sharply. Standing in front of her was a large, handsome man. He was looking at her through dark glasses; she couldn't see his eyes, and she wondered if he was looking at her with the usual . . . and it crossed her mind that she hadn't had her hair cut; she must do it. Then she noticed that in the man's right hand was a white stick. He was blind.

"It was my fault, I'm so sorry, I was walking along with my head down because of the rain and I just didn't see you," said Carmichael. She felt that was a tactless remark, but the man did not appear to take it so.

He replied genially, "I see, but it isn't often I have the chance to hold a pretty girl in my arms, even for a second." He smiled, and the charming voice and his demeanour took all the suggestion of freshness or boldness out of the remark.

Carmichael said again, "It was really my fault. Are you all right now?"

The man nodded vigorously. "I always go home from the university this way. Good evening," he said. He stepped out firmly, his stick held slightly in front of him. Carmichael watched him go, watched him turn the corner at the church and disappear.

"It's not often I get the chance to hold a pretty girl in my arms," he had said, and somehow that remark blotted out everything else from Carmichael's mind. The priest, the confessional, everything except the blind man's voice and the feeling of his strong arms round her. She got into her car, still thinking of him, and drove home to her flat, her television, and her cat.

About the Author

Anthea Cohen trained as a nurse at Leicester Royal Infirmary. For the past twenty-five years she has worked, on and off, in hospitals and as a private nurse. She has written on medicine and hospital life, has been a columnist for *Nursing Mirror,* and has contributed regularly to *World Medicine.* She has published innumerable short stories and is a popular author of books for the teenage market in the United States. *Angel of Vengeance* follows *Angel Without Mercy* in the Crime Club.